Messenger

A Jaegers of the Consortium Novel

by
Diesel Jester

Jaegers of the Consortium Series:
Shadow
Cheyenne
Messenger

Messenger: A Jaegers of the Consortium novel

ISBN: 978-1-939473-87-5
Copyright © 2018 by Diesel Jester
All rights reserved.
Printed and bound in the United States of America.
Steam Paperback Edition: October 2018
Steam is a division of Kennebec Publishing, LLC

For all my sisters; step, in-law, adopted, or otherwise.
Don't let your older brother corrupt you too much...

"For he shall give his angels charge over you, to keep you in all your ways."
-Psalms: Chapter 91, Verse 11.

Acknowledgements

Special thanks to John G. Hemry (AKA: Jack Campbell) for his insights into the model and rules set that he used for starship combat and how they could be applied to airship combat.

Thank you to my beta readers:
    Crystal Larkin
    Sabrina Hootman

Thank you to my beta editors:
    Lady Katheryne
    Julia Hennagir

Thank you to my cover models who agreed to do the photoshoot:
    Thomas Dean Willeford
    Amy Wilder

Cover photography by:
    Chad Geist, Omni Lens Studios

And thank you to all of my family, friends, and fans who waited for so long for this book!

CHAPTER 1

In the 83rd year of the Consortium...

Lucilla "Lucy" Spence, Baroness of Alpharetta, hummed quietly to herself as she moved around the dressing room, unpacking her valise for what she expected to be a lovely and relaxing weekend in Atlanta. At twenty-one, and unmarried, she seldom got the chance to have unchaperoned time. Well, unchaperoned as long as you didn't count the vSlave her bother insisted go along with her at all times to handle the financing of her activities. Eddie never trusted her with things, especially something as important as money. Despite that, she was determined not to let her family's rules, or societal etiquette, ruin her stay in the city. The Georgian Regis was the grandest hotel in all of Atlanta, if not the entire Theocracy of Dixie, and that was a treat to be savored.

She was just stowing her parasol when a tall, red-haired woman brandishing a beamer suddenly burst through her front door and into the dressing room. Giving a startled squeak, Lucy spun around and swung wildly at the intruder with the parasol. The woman laughed, dodged the swipe, and pointed the beamer at her.

"Down on the floor, now!" she commanded.

Seeing there was no other choice, when bringing an umbrella to a beamer fight, Lucy sank to the floor. She scooted back as much as her corseted dress would allow. Doing the only thing her frantic mind could conjure, she flicked the locking mechanism on her parasol, hoping that somehow the silk and lace would miraculously stop a beamer bolt. The slight metallic click was followed by a soft *schooop* sound as the parasol opened to form a makeshift shield. Lucy, though thoroughly terrified, laughed at the ridiculousness of her situation.

The smug redhead called over her shoulder. "Got her! Dressing room next to the bedroom, come straight in from the front door!"

She then smirked down at Lucy. "My mother always said that it's bad luck to open an umbrella indoors."

"It's a parasol, not an umbrella," Lucy retorted without thinking and then blanched when the intruder laughed at her.

Two men, followed by a blonde vSlave walked in. "Well, meet our big, badass, criminal mind." The redhead gestured down at Lucy.

"No," said the tall, dark man who was clearly leading the others. He shook his head. "There's more to it than just this."

Lucy risked a peek from behind her parasol and saw that he was examining her with questioning dark eyes.

"What's your name?" he asked, his tone surprisingly calm and gentle.

"L-Lucy... Lucy Spence. I'm the daughter of Count-Reverend Edward Spence. Please... please leave! Please don't hurt me. I-I'll call security and the Consortium on you!"

"We *are* the Consortium, honey," the second man said. He pulled opened his duster. There, where his left breast pocket would be, Lucy saw a bronze star set within a silver cog. The silver ID plate underneath read *Jaeger Deliverer*.

A Jaeger? Here? Why? Lucy thought in alarm. "But—I haven't done anything wrong!" she protested.

"Eddie's little sister?" the vSlave girl in the doorway asked, the shock evident in her voice. "Are you in on this, too?"

Lucy peeked farther around the edge of the parasol to get her first look at the vSlave. *Oh my Lord*, Lucy thought, *is that who I think it is?*

"Charity?" she asked, confused as to why the eldest Carmichael daughter, and fiancée to her own brother, was here. "In on what? Eddie said things were tense at home, so he sent me here to the city for a week while he went around taking care of business."

Eyes narrowing, the dark-haired man with the cane looked at Lucy. "Where's your servant, the man who's been seen with you whenever you're in public?"

"Esmond? He's downstairs, taking care of the bill. He handles the finances when I come into Atlanta." Lucy frowned.

"What?" Charity asked, sounding furious.

Lucy's eyes went wide, and even the men seemed shocked as Charity lunged her way. The mysterious man

2

grabbed her around the waist and held her back as she cried, "You lying little trollop! Esmond works for my family!"

"What—what are you talking about?" Lucy's eyes were big, and she held her parasol even tighter.

"He has been ever since your family sold his contract to us. Eddie loans him out from time to time, but he still belongs to us."

Still holding Charity, the man whirled toward Deliverer and the redhead, jerking his thumb back toward the elevators. "Get him," he said, and they both nodded, rushing from the room. "Okay, Miss Spence," the dark man said, offering his free hand to Lucy. Charity was quieting, and he let her down, but kept a hand on her arm. "How about we go into the sitting room and try to sort this out, hmm?"

Lucy looked up at him, down at his hand, and back up again. "My brother said that I shouldn't talk to anyone without him, or Esmond, or our family's attorney present. For—for propriety's sake."

The man sighed, and pushed a hand through his black hair. "Fair enough," he said, trying to keep his voice calm. "We can have a call put in to the Spence family attorney, and you can tell them you've been arrested on suspicion of fraud, identity theft, and grand larceny. They can collect you at the Consortium regional office here, downtown. I'm sure your family will be delighted to come bail you out. You'll be the talk of the town for months."

Lucy's shuddered. The scandal would be unbearable and she wouldn't be allowed to enter the courting season this coming fall alongside her own new fiancée if such a thing happened!

The man smiled. "Fret not, the trial won't take long. We have enough evidence and eyewitness statements to put you away for a good long time. And a woman like you? So young? So beautiful? You'll be very popular in the prison system as a comfort girl. Or, you could opt into iron-slave status, and go to some crusty, old gentleman at the public auctions. Up to you."

He was silent for a moment, and then held his hand out for her, gently. "Or, you can come to the sitting room with me, right now, just for a minute, and answer my very simple,

3

very informal questions without my having to officially charge you. What do you say?"

That was far worse a fate than a mere scandal. She could not bear the thought of being forced into slavery in such a way. Seeing no other solution, Lucy drew her chin up, and looked him stoically in the eye. "The sitting room would be preferable."

With as much grace and dignity the situation would allow, Lucy let the man help her to her feet and escort her to the sitting room.

"When did you make yourself blonde?" Charity asked once they were seated. "You used to have really pretty red hair."

Lucy looked at the collar around Charity's neck, then away. "Must she be here," she asked with a hushed voice. "I don't want to say this in front of a slave." She'd always been taught that slaves talk, and did not want information leaking out, former aristocrat or not. She didn't know why Charity wore a collar now, but it didn't matter.

"What?" Charity gasped.

"Well, you are wearing a collar now, strangely enough. That means you're—"

"My slave, not yours," the man cut in. "And my call. Answer the question, please; I'm intrigued, now that she's mentioned it."

"Oh, alright," Lucy lowered her eyes. "Earlier this year, I think it was right before Charity came back from University, Eddie mentioned how much better I would look if I were a blonde and so I decided that I'd try it out for this season." Lucy patted and fluffed her hair. "I think it looks good on me. What are your thoughts on this, Mr.... oh, I'm sorry... I didn't catch your name?"

"No, you didn't," the man said. "So, you never questioned the fact that you look remarkably like Charity here from a distance? Nor was it suspicious to you that a house slave, formerly belonging to the Carmichaels and often on loan to them, suddenly became your escort for whenever you were in Atlanta?"

"Why would it be? It hardly matters where a slave comes from," Lucy said. "Is it not the same where you live?"

Lucy had never been allowed out of the Theocracy, nor did her homeschool education ever allow her the opportunity to read about life in other nations.

"Let's just say that we don't make it a habit of buying slaves from someone and then leaving them in the house we'd just purchased them from."

"Esmond had been with the Carmichaels for years prior to us buying out his contract. There was no sense in moving him from where he was." *Especially if we were going to join with said family when Eddie marries Charity,* Lucy mentally added.

"Excuse me if I maintain a bit of skepticism, here," the dark man said.

All three of them turned to look at the front door of the suite when Esmond suddenly walked in, interrupting them.

"Esmond!" Charity exclaimed as she shot to her feet.

Esmond's eyes went wide when he saw her, and he began to turn and run, but was instead backed into the nearest wall as Charity advanced on him.

"Tell me that you were not a part of this! Tell me this was all just a big mistake! Tell me that you were not stealing my money, my family's money!" Charity cried out.

Esmond's mouth opened and closed, gaping like a fish, visibly shocked by her presence and her parasol now pointed at him like a sword.

The dark man grabbed her and pulled her back before she got the idea to run Esmond through. "Easy, dear, let's see what he has to say first."

"I want to know the truth! Why are you betraying us?" Charity cried out, struggling in the man's grip. "We trusted you! We took care of you! Why?"

Esmond opened his mouth to speak but then inched back toward the doors. When Deliverer and the redhead came busting back in, he slumped in defeat. "I'm sorry, Miss Charity," he said, head bowed in shame. "I had to do it. But, only to pay off my debts! To get out of indentured servitude! My brother promised me I would be freed if I went along with Mr. Spence's plan. The Baron wanted to ruin your family and bring them into the Spence household as servants."

"And who's your brother?" Jaeger Deliverer demanded,

positioning himself next to the man. He fished a pair of handcuffs from the leather pouch on his thigh and proceeded to cuff the man.

"Ambrose Wain."

"Oh, this keeps getting better," the dark man mused. "Alright, take him and Lucy down to the Consortium offices and put them in lockup." He pointed at the two of them. "Cooperate fully by helping us bring down Eddie and Ambrose and we can try and get you a deal. If not, you'll be prosecuted right alongside them." He looked at Deliverer. "Get them out of here."

"Are you going to take their statements?" Deliverer asked.

"No," the dark man shook his head. "You do it. I have bigger fish to fry. Read him his rights and get him processed."

"With what charge?" Esmond asked, aghast.

"We'll go with theft, embezzlement, and obfuscation of fund movement for starters and work our way up from there."

"You heard the man," Deliverer said, turning on Lucy and Esmond. He pointed toward the door. "March."

As she was herded out the door by the Jaeger alongside of her family's slave, Lucy leaned in toward Esmond. "What have you and my brother done?" she deman-ded.

"I'd be quiet, if I were you," the redheaded woman said.

"And you are?" Lucy retorted.

"None of your concern," Deliverer interrupted the whisperings. "Esmond Wain, Lucy Spence, you both are hereby under arrest on the charges listed by Consortium official Lucas Wolverton just now. You both have the right to remain silent as anything you say or do can and will be used against you in a court of law. As this is a matter of the Consortium, you both have the right to contact your country's consulate for advice and/or an advocate. If your country cannot or will not provide an advocate, and you cannot afford one yourself, then one will be appointed to you by the Consortium to represent you during questioning. Do you understand these rights as they have been dictated to you?"

"Yes," Esmond said with resignation.

"Wait! The dark man in there... er... Official Wolverton was it... said that I was just going to give statements," Lucy

6

said in a near panic, her breathing accelerating. She started to feel faint.

"Do you understand these rights as they have been dictated to you?" Deliverer repeated.

"Y-yes," Lucy stammered before being led away.

***

"Henry Tandey, Old Calendar of 1918 at the height of the Great War," Gabriel McKibben, the Messenger, said as he clicked the slide that depicted a British Private of the time period. He was addressing his class in the Atlanta Consortium Academy, and stroked his sandy-colored beard as he paced in front of the theater. "Considered by many to be the first Jaeger after he single-handedly held down a position near Marcoing, France against advancing Germans. He stayed his hand against one German Lance Corporal who was mortally wounded in the firefight and even rendered this man aid. Now, we do not know the name of this German or what he would've become, but we do know that Tandey went on to serve the rest of the war in a hunter fashion, systematically taking out opposing forces while at the same time rendering aid to the fallen."

Gabriel clicked to the next slide, the cog-and-star symbol of the Jaeger Corps in which he served. "That's what it means to be a Jaeger: You will be the Consortium's military arm to bring justice to those who oppress the weak, while at the same time offering the hand of mercy to those who are unable to fight back." He lifted a single finger to emphasize his point as he quoted. "'He will bring into judgement both the righteous and the wicked, for there will be a time for every activity and a time to judge every deed....' Ecclesiastes Chapter Three, Verse Seventeen, from the One Book that is held dear here within the Theocracy of Dixie. Only it will not be the Lord's judgement that you bring down—it will be the Consortium's."

While his students took notes, he saw someone motioning from the door to his left. It was Hector Murphy, and by his stern expression, this was going to take up the rest of his time today.

7

Gabriel acknowledged him with a nod, and then turned back to his class. "Chapter five for tomorrow—'End of the Great War and Geneva Intervention.' That's all for today."

The students collected their things and filed out while Gabriel went over to his boss, who was patiently waiting by the door. "What's up, Goliath?"

Hector, head of operations in Atlanta, handed him a dossier and motioned for him to follow. "I need an advocate for a case. No one from the Theocracy will touch it," he said without preamble as was his normal way of operating. "Rich daughter of the Theocracy is being brought in with her manservant for questioning. He already has an advocate, but she doesn't."

"That's weird...," Gabriel muttered, glancing over the notes. "Esmond Wain... iSlave to... are you fucking kidding me? The Spences? Seriously?" He eyed Hector, wondering if this was a joke.

Hector nodded solemnly. "Esmond is the brother of one of the most influential Directors of Banks here in Atlanta and knows family secrets that can bring both families down. He was given the Wain family advocate first while the daughter is being hung out to dry. The Spence family advocate is already being tasked to the eldest family son in anticipation of his arrest."

"Which daughter...?" Gabriel flipped through the dossier until he came to the information. He stopped in his tracks. "Oh... God...." The eyes of his old flame... his old fiancé, no less stared back at him. He'd buried Lucy Spence's memory into the distant past and now here she was, returning to his life again. "Oh, Lucy... what did your family do this time, girl?" he wondered out loud.

"Pissed Shadow off," Hector replied with an amused snort. "Shadow is going after Eddie Spence while he sent Deliverer our way with Lucy and Esmond in tow. They've been systematically draining the Carmichael accounts dry. We don't know the motivations... yet. That's Deliverer's job. Your job is to act as Miss Spence's advocate."

"No."

Hector regarded him with a disdainful eyebrow. "Really?" he asked.

8

Gabriel realized that this wasn't a request, but he couldn't possibly do what was being demanded of him. "I must recuse myself. We have a history."

"You're the best I've got and you and I both know that the Theocracy is going to railroad her," Hector pointed out. "This comes down from Shadow himself. He wants her to have good representation in the courts, thinks she's caught in the middle of something bigger."

When Gabriel went to speak, Hector held up a hand. "You're a Jaeger; you're expected to maintain neutrality no matter what, and I expect you to defend her to the best of your ability."

Gabriel closed the dossier and handed it back to him. "I respectfully request that you get someone else who is just as good as you think I am. Huntress..."

"In Elysium," Hector countered.

"Defender?"

"In the Corporate States and locked in litigation until the end of the year."

"Jurist?"

"In another lawsuit against the Theocracy again," Hector said and sighed.

"Hell, go out west and reinstate Angel for all I care!"

"Fuck you!" Hector gave him a disdainful look, finally fed up. "I'd eat a goddamn airship full of Tisigen rather than get him! Face it—you're the best I have, you're the best I have right now, and you have the case."

With that, Hector gave him a curt nod and peeled off in another direction, leaving Gabriel to look over the dossier and contemplate his latest assignment.

"What the hell has your family done now, girl?" he wondered again as he stared at Lucy's bright eyes and equally bright smile.

CHAPTER 2

Out of all the girls to get assigned to,
I get this one...

Gabriel thought ruefully as he looked through the glass of the one-way mirror into the interrogation room. On the other side, Lucy Spence sat at the table in an immaculate white blouse underneath a brown corset, sitting prim and proper as always, with her hands folded on her lap. Since getting here from the academy, he'd had time to think about what had happened to their relationship all those years ago. Part of him wondered if Lucy even remembered him, she had been so young and it was so long ago. He shook off his doubt. They *were* engaged briefly, after all. That's not an easy detail to omit from one's memory. Part of him also wondered if she remembered the atrocities that her father was responsible for, or if she and her younger sister had been sheltered away from that aspect of the family. He glanced at his notes and the dossier again and then looked at his fellow Jaeger standing next to him, Jake Walker... Deliverer. Jake eyed him right back.

"You up for this?" he asked.

"The question is—are you?" Gabriel responded.

Once he walked into the interrogation room to be Lucy's advocate, he'd mop the floor with Jake. Jake was good and made the arrests, but he was headstrong and hardheaded when it came to questioning people. It was a tactic that would get the younger Jaeger into trouble one of these days.

"So... run me through this one more time and tell me what her family is being accused of and why she's here," Gabriel said with a deep breath as he continued to study his ex-fiancé through the one-way mirror.

"Edward Spence the Third is engaged to Charity Carmichael," Jake responded without hesitation. "Lucy Spence, here, has been gallivanting across Atlanta using Miss Carmichael's accounts that were given to her by her brother. She's been caught on flasher pics posing as Charity. Their vSlave, Esmond, is owned by the Spences but is keeping tabs on the Carmichaels... his former owners. Lucas Wolverton found that Charity's accounts were being drained despite a Consortium hold being put on it because—"

"Because they had an inside man at the bank to keep the accounts open regardless," Gabriel finished the sentence for him. He gave Jake a sideways smile. "It's not the first time the Spences tried this song and dance. It looks like they finally got their hand caught in the cookie jar." Gabriel snorted in amusement at Jake's confused look. "They did the same thing to my family. Why pay an insanely high bride price for a noblewoman here in the Theocracy when you can just bankrupt their family and force them into servitude?"

Jake gasped, blinking in astonishment. "They're forcing people into illegal slavery?"

"Yeah, but they get away with it because it goes unreported," Gabriel said and nodded sagely. "This is the Theocracy, kid. Where have you been all this time? Women go by what the men tell them, and if they tell them to shut the hell up on pain of everything up to, but not quite including death, then they do it." Gabriel tapped his chin in thought. "If the Spences are following their standard procedure, then they were going to force Charity Carmichael into vSlave status under Eddie Spence at an insanely low rate, he'd marry her, then they'd make a play for the Carmichael assets."

"Which is what happened to your family?" Jake prodded. He was taking notes now.

Gabriel nodded. "Charity isn't Eddie's first fiancé. My sister was."

The grief still ate at him just thinking about it. She'd been so young and sweet, only eighteen. At the same time, to cement relations between the Spence house and the McKibben house, Gabriel had been promised to Lucy, him being twenty-five and she just as old as his sister. Now here they all were, ten years later, going at it again. "By the time we knew what was happening, it was all over. I just barely managed to get some of the family assets transferred away so that the Spences couldn't get them before going into hiding."

"Damn...," Jake whistled. "And now you're stuck defending one aspect of the family responsible for your own downfall."

11

"Yeah... fuck my life...."

***

It had been a couple of hours since her arrest and Lucy paced nervously in the interrogation room between bouts of sitting. and wringing her hands nervously. The moment she got to the Constabulary House in Atlanta where the Jaegers operated from in her country, she put in a call in to her father for assistance.

"I'll see what I can do," was all his gruff voice said back to her.

That was two long hours ago, and Lucy was at her wits' end. Had her father forsaken her? Was she to be left to the mercy of the courts? She wrung her hands as she paced with her thoughts going crazy.

The door to the interrogation room opened and a tall, muscular, dirty blonde-haired man in an immaculate gentleman's suit walked in.

"Good evening, Miss Spence, my name is Gabriel McKibben. I go by Jaeger Messenger within the Consortium." He said formally, showing her his badge before sticking his hand out to her.

Lucy stared at him, shocked by the sight of the man in front of her. "Gabe...," she breathed in disbelief. Following the training of her youth, she politely held out her shaking gloved hand to him and he kissed the back of her knuckles. The bristles of his sandy beard and moustache tickled even through her thin gloves.

Gabriel remained stoic, holding his hand in place and ignoring her shocked statement. "By joint agreement between the Theocracy of Dixie and the Consortium, I am your court-appointed advocate for these proceedings." Under his left arm, he carried a briefcase that he promptly sat on the table beside her.

"My advocate... A Jaeger?" Lucy blinked. "*You*? What happened to my family's advocate? I called my father!" She couldn't believe what was happening.

"Yeah... that...." Gabriel looked apologetic. "Your family's advocate has already been tasked to defend your brother once

12

the investigation team brings him in. Your house slave, Esmond, has had an advocate appointed by his brother, Ambrose. Your father was unable to get another advocate from Dixie for you since word of what your brother is up to has already spread like wildfire and no one is willing to even touch your family right now. Thus, you get me." He pulled out a chair for her at the table and motioned for her to sit.

"But, aren't you supposed to be an investigator and enforcer?" Lucy asked, confused, but fluttering out her skirts so that she could sit comfortably. "Why would a Jaeger be my advocate?"

"It's my area of specialization when I'm not encased in brass armor. Yes, yes, I know all the rumors. As a Jaeger, I can kill a man five ways and pleasure a woman five more, using only my thumb. I kill the bad guys and bed the good girls, yadda, yadda, yadda...."

Lucy felt herself blush at his mention of pleasuring women. It caught her off guard and she did her best to remain composed but knew he could see her slight discomfort. She felt embarrassed, suddenly resentful of her innocence and propriety.

"At any rate, shall we get started?" he asked, sitting down next to her.

Lucy's cheeks flushed even hotter when he sat so close to her, but she felt relief that he was ready to change the subject. "Shouldn't you be on the other end, Mr. McKibben?" she asked.

"No, that seat is for Jake."

"Jake?"

"Sorry. Jake Walker; Jaeger Deliverer." Gabriel said as he opened his briefcase. "The Jaeger who arrested you and is conducting the investigation."

Lucy frowned. "I'm sorry, but you can't possibly represent me. Isn't that a conflict?" She tried to come up with the sound reason. "You... me... er... we... I mean, aren't you two supposed to be on the same team?"

***

Gabriel laughed as he pulled out a sheaf of paper and a pen.

"We are in on the same team in that we both ensure justice is done correctly. So, he will ask you questions as it pertains to his case and I will ensure fair treatment for you. Now, before I get him in here, is there anything I need to know regarding the circumstances of your arrest?"

"Yes!" Lucy practically blurted out. "I was told by a Consortium official, a Mr. Wolf... Wolverton... I believe that's what his name was? I just got wind of it as I was being hustled out the door. I was told that I was just going to answer some questions in exchange for a deal and that I was not being arrested!"

"Really? That's interesting," Gabriel said, taking down notes on his pad as she talked. "They didn't mention that in the briefing. Anything else? What was your arrest all about?"

"Didn't you say that you were briefed on it?"

"Yes, but I want to hear it from you to make sure that I have all sides of the story."

"Fine," Lucy said and recounted the strange happening at her suite earlier in the day. Gabriel remained quiet, taking notes save for the occasional question for clarification.

"Okay. I think that we're ready now." He stood up and walked to the door, nodding at someone on the other end, before heading back to his seat next to Lucy.

Moments later, Jake Walker came in and engaged the voice recorder in the corner of the room. Gears clanked and there were a few clicks and whirrs as the machine powered up. Once he was satisfied that everything was in order, Jake came back to the table to sit opposite Lucy and Gabriel.

"For the record," Jake said formally, reading from his notes, "this is the interrogation of Baroness Lucille Faith Spence. Arrested this twelfth day of July, Consortium Year Eighty-Three. To sum up the charges, Miss Spence is accused of willful collaboration with her brother, Edward Spence the Third; her house slave, Esmond Wain; and Regional Bank Director Ambrose Wain; of embezzlement, obfuscation of funds, and grand larceny. Miss Spence, do you have counsel present?"

"Um, yes, I do. I was told that Jaeger Messenger is my Advocate in this matter." Lucy replied, eyes darting to Gabriel who nodded at her.

"And, Miss Spence, are you still aware of your rights as they have been told to you?"

"Yes, I am."

"And, with your Advocate present, are you willing to answer my questions?"

"Yes."

"Good," Jake said and gave her a feral, predatory smile. "Now, what is your relationship to Baron Edward Spence the Third?"

Gabriel leaned forward. "Before she answers that question, my client has been offered a deal by a Consortium official in the course of this investigation. This offer, one of immunity in exchange for testimony, was given prior to her arrest and done in full view of yourself and two other witnesses, correct?" He glared at Jake as if daring him to contradict him.

Jake's jaw worked as Gabriel spoke. "Yes, that is correct," he said tersely.

"So, I want your oath, on the record, that all charges against my client be dropped before she answers a single question."

Jake folded his hands and looked Gabriel in the eye. "Your client has collaborated—"

"*Allegedly*, collaborated, you mean?" Gabriel corrected with a single upraised finger.

"Yes... allegedly collaborated... with Baron Spence," Jake sighed. "If she talks, we can offer immunity."

Lucy watched the verbal exchange with hope in her chest. She had her doubts about Gabriel properly defending her, but those doubts quickly evaporated as he went after Jake in full force. She did a quick double take when Gabriel motioned for her to lean in close to him.

"I'm sure I already know the answer to this, but I just like making investigators stew for a bit. But, I also need your verbal consent to make everything official. Will you tell him everything you know about your involvement and what your brother and house slave have been up to in exchange for an immunity agreement?"

"Yes, of course." Lucy nodded emphatically.

"Now you do realize, of course, that you might be called

to testify against your brother, don't you?"

That was something that Lucy was not expecting. Testify? In court? Against her own brother? What was the old saying about a house divided against itself could not stand? She couldn't possibly do that. Was she even *allowed* to do that here? But, then again, she was also compelled by sacred law, handed down by God, to comply with any legal authority. As much as it pained her, she finally nodded. After all, God's word compelled her to comply with lawful authority.

"Alright then," Gabriel said with a nod. "Let's get moving on this." He straightened up and looked at Jake with all seriousness. "My client agrees on the stipulation that all charges are dropped after this questioning is over. Agreed?"

"Agreed." Jake nodded. "Now, Miss Spence, do you know why you're here?"

"Irrelevant and open-ended question designed to trap my client," Gabriel snapped irritably. "Keep on topic to your investigation, if you please?"

"Fine." Jake shot an ugly look at him before returning his focus back to Lucy. "We'll go back to my first question: what is your relation to Edward Spence the Third?"

"He's my brother."

"Through blood?"

"No, she just calls him that for the hell of it. Deliverer, move on!" Gabriel said disdainfully.

Jake frowned at Gabriel and then looked at his notes. "For the past year, you have been posing as Charity Carmichael of Marietta, using her accounts under her name. Is this correct?"

"What?" Lucy reeled back in shock. "Heavens, no! Why would I?"

"So, you deny posing as her, then?" When Jake caught Gabriel's withering glare, he quickly held up his hand and moved on. "I withdraw the question. Regardless, you look a lot like her with your hair dyed blonde like that," Jake pointed out. He took a pic out and slid it across the table for her and Gabriel to see. "This flasher pic was taken of you at the Regional Bank of Dixie last week when you and Esmond were meeting with his brother, Ambrose, who happens to be the branch manager."

"How do we know that's not Charity Carmichael herself?" Gabriel noted. "The pic quality is poor and one can barely make out any facial features."

"Because I have three primary eyewitness accounts that place her in Elysium at the time, along with airship tickets, as well as statements from the Carmichaels themselves." Jake saw Gabriel about to protest and he held up a forestalling hand again. "The eyewitnesses are myself, Lucas Wolverton of the accounting section of the Consortium Regional Headquarters, and Ayla Greenstar who is a businesswoman and the daughter of the founders of Greenstar Industries."

Gabriel leaned in close to Lucy. "You've got to tell me right now—is this you or not?"

"It is me, but... but...," Lucy said, feeling her panic rising. "Might I explain?"

Gabriel nodded and motioned for her to do so.

Lucy straightened up and squared her shoulders. "Every time I came to Atlanta to take in a show, or go shopping, or whatever, Esmond always met me here in the city. He, on my brother's authority, always handled the money issues. No woman of good breeding would handle money herself—it's dirty. Propriety is paramount. Otherwise, it might affect...," she looked at Gabriel and flinched, "my marriage prospects. This particular day, we were there because he needed to speak with the bank on some trouble that he was having with the accounts. Someone had put a hold on them and tried to have them completely frozen."

"I see," Jake said, taking notes. "Did you ever see which accounts were being used?"

"No! Eddie told me to always let Esmond handle it and I do what my elder brother says."

"Charity Carmichael said that you used to be a redhead," Jake said, shifting tracks. "When did you dye your hair blonde?"

"About a year ago."

"Who suggested that you do it?"

"Eddie."

"That didn't strike you as odd?"

Lucy shrugged. "He said that gentlemen were going for blondes lately and wanted me seen out in public prior to me

17

being declared to my fiancé this coming fall." She dared another look at Gabriel and, lowering her head, she softly continued. "I followed what my older brother had suggested that I do."

"Which we all know that, per Theocracy law, any 'suggestion' given by a senior male of the household can be taken as an order by any female, regardless of age," Gabriel interjected. "Had Baron Spencer the Third suggested it to his own mother, she would've had no choice but to do so."

Jake nodded once. "Yes, I am in agreement with that assessment." He scribbled down some notes. "Miss Spence, had Eddie ever once told you of his plans with Charity Carmichael?"

"A... a bit," Lucy admitted. "He told me that it was his intention to marry her and take over controlling the finances of the Carmichaels as it would be a big boost to both of our houses. The Carmichael's aircraft factories alone would make us the richest house in the country."

Jake smiled and gestured to her. "Please, continue," he said.

***

Standing on the witness dais in the center of the courtroom, Lucy concluded her testimony against her own brother. Despite her nerves and misgivings, she spoke loud and clear to the judge before her and answered the same questions as she had a couple of days earlier.

"I had no knowledge that my brother was having me conduct activities under the disguise of Charity Carmichael, nor did I have any knowledge that he had our house slave, Esmond Wain, make transactions on my behalf under her name," she said, unable to hide her newfound disgust for Eddie. She glanced over to him, as he sat in the space for the accused, barely able to disguise her contempt. He remained stony-faced and silent as he glared right back at her.

In the space of a couple of days, he had not only been discovered for all the crimes that he had dragged her into, but he had also pulled a knife and a beamer on the same Consortium official who she'd talked with, kidnapped Charity

Carmichael out of petty revenge, and then proceeded to beat the poor girl almost to death. Today, Lucy was ashamed to be called a Spence. This was not how father had raised them.

"Had I known what he was up to, I would have put an end to it at once as I am uncomfortable being an instrument that contributed to the downfall of a prominent house within our country," Lucy concluded.

The witness' dais was flanked by Jaegers Deliverer and Messenger who were serving as Prosecutor and Advocate, respectively, and then her brother and his advocate to her left. Lucy averted her eyes from her brother, as she could hardly look at Eddie's seething glare.

She was the last witness to be called and her testimony was the last in a pile of already damning evidence that the Consortium had brought against him. Lucy had sat through the testimonies of Lucas Wolverton, Charity Carmichael, Ayla Greenstar, another Jaeger, a few constables, the count and countess of Marietta themselves, Esmond, and a host of accountants from the bank.

"Thank you, Miss Spence," Jake said with a nod before turning to look up at the judge who was seated behind his bench, elevated above everyone else. "The Consortium has no further questions for this witness."

"Advocate?" the judge asked, looking toward Gabriel.

"The advocate for the witness has no further questions, and we move that the Consortium make good on the agreement reached earlier in the week that led to the arrest warrant of the accused," Gabriel said, standing up from behind his desk.

"The Consortium has no objection with this motion, your Honor," Jake said.

"Objection, your Honor!" Michael Ladd—Eddie's advocate—called out from the opposite side of the room. "Advocate for the defense has yet to cross-examine!"

"Irrelevant, your Honor. Miss Lucy Spence is not the one on trial here," Gabriel countered, raising his voice. "Whatever deal was made with the Consortium does not affect her testimony or her ability to be questioned during these proceedings."

"Overruled," the judge said. "Per the agreement made in

exchange for testimony, the charges against Baroness Lucy Spence are hereby dismissed. Defense advocate, you may proceed with your cross-examination."

Lucy let out a sigh of relief. It was almost over and now she was officially free! She steeled herself against her own family's ruthless advocate who had a spotless win record. Then again, he'd contended against a pair of Jaegers before, and the amount of concrete evidence they produced was staggering.

"Miss Spence," Mr. Ladd said, admonishing her with a hard glare as the Jaegers took their seats at the prosecution table. "You are a citizen of the Theocracy, are you not?" he asked in a stern tone.

"Yes," Lucy replied cautiously. Her gaze flickered to Gabriel and he, too, was warily watching Ladd. Their eyes met and he gave her a slight nod, motioning to continue answering his questions. During trial preparation, she learned that, at any time, Gabriel could step in and end the line of questioning if Ladd tried to get Lucy in trouble. She took a deep breath, confident that this would all be over very soon.

Ladd folded his hands in front of Lucy and looked down his nose at her. "As such, does not the Theocracy state that you are not to bear witness against your own family unless you have permission from a male in your family?"

Gabriel and Jake were both on their feet at once, shouting out their objections. "This is Consortium matter!" Gabriel bellowed out first. "Theocracy law does not apply here!"

"The advocate for the defense cannot cite nationality in his line of questioning, as it bears no relevance for this case!" Jake roared just as loud.

Ladd held up a hand in surrender. "I withdraw the question, your Honor," he said softly. He pressed his wire-frame glasses up the bridge of his nose before continuing. He folded his hands again and gave Lucy a patronizing smile. "Miss Spence, you have a history of very liberal spending with your own family funds, do you not?" He glanced at the Jaegers, who were both ready to pounce by shouting more objections. "It goes for the credibility of the witness!" he snapped and raised a forestalling hand before they could say anything.

Lucy figured that if looks could kill, then Ladd would've been dead on the spot by the way that both Jaegers were glaring at him. She swallowed hard. "No more than any other member of Dixie aristocracy," she said, trying to keep the dignified tone in her voice from wavering.

Cocking his head thoughtfully, Ladd looked at her and she felt herself whither under his hard gaze. "So, would it be safe to say that your spending habits would've caused your *older* brother to do something rash, like tap into other funding sources to sustain your spending habits?"

"Objection!" Jake called out, jumping to his feet. "Leading the witness!"

"If I may have permission to treat the witness as hostile?" Ladd asked the judge innocently.

"Why?" Gabriel chimed in. "She's from *your employer's* family!"

"Because if you haven't noticed, brother and sister are not exactly seeing eye to eye, here," Ladd said as he motioned over to his client. "She has officially broken with the family by bearing witness against an older family member," he said somberly. "Her father has refused to provide her with any support in this matter, which is the reason why *you* are sitting there, Messenger," he added with his own glare toward the Jaeger.

Lucy blinked and felt a bit faint. *Broken with the family? Father cut me off?* Lucy thought with alarm. *No! I have done no such thing! How can he say that?*

"Objection overruled," the judge admitted. "Permission granted to treat as a hostile witness," he said while Gabriel muttered a few choice phrases under his breath as to Ladd's parentage.

What does that mean? Lucy wondered as she looked uncertainly from the judge, to Ladd, then over to Gabriel. She mouthed the words "help me" to him as she had no idea what was coming next.

"Permission to approach?" Gabriel called out. At the judge's nod, he cleared the distance between them. He motioned for her to lean over and he whispered into her ear.

"He's allowed to challenge your testimony and ask very leading questions without regard to prior evidence submitted. I have no idea what he's up to with his line of questioning, so be careful with your answers."

"O-Okay." Lucy nodded. She swallowed hard again to steady her nerves.

"Relax and take a couple of deep breaths. You're doing fine. Jake and I will try and keep him off your back as much as we can." Gabriel gave her a reassuring smile and patted her hand in a friendly manner. She found herself blushing and smiling back at him.

"If you're done flirting with the witness?" Ladd asked with disdain. "She has a husband arranged."

"Funny how he's not here and you're treating her like a common criminal, then," Gabriel shot back with equal hostility. "Get on with your line of questioning." He patted his sidearm. "Just be careful of where you go or else you'll be finding out if you do have a higher power or not."

"Counsel will refrain from shooting opposing counsel," the judge said with an eyeroll and a resigned sigh.

"Can I just wing him, then?" Gabriel asked innocently, grinning while he sat back down.

CHAPTER 3

The trial ended and Lucy forced herself to watch as the judge read out the verdict. She looked around and found it odd that Mother and Father were not here to lend their support. For that matter, even the Carmichaels were not in attendance but she'd heard that Charity was still recovering from the beating she'd received from Eddie. Lucy couldn't help but shudder at the memory of seeing Charity Carmichael, days earlier, as she walked to the witness dais with as much honor and dignity that she could muster despite her injuries. After her testimony, Lucy made it a point to head out to the lobby and apologize profusely for how she'd treated her back at the Regis.

"I am so sorry, had I only known," Lucy gushed.

Charity gave her a sad smile. "It's okay. Really. You now have other things to worry about. Try not to let your brother bring you down."

Now, it was nearly a week after Eddie had been arrested. From what she'd heard, justice moved a lost faster these days than it did prior to the Cataclysm. Maybe that was why her parents were not here. With all the evidence and testimony presented, Eddie's fate was almost certain. In fact, the audience was sparsely populated with a few Consortium clerks who were taking notes along with one stony-faced prison overseer who seemed to regard Lucy with great curiosity.

When Eddie was called up to the dais for judgement and sentencing, someone slid into the chair next to her in the courtroom audience. "You shouldn't be here for this."

It was Gabriel and he put a hand on her hand, which had a white-knuckled grip of the arm of the chair. "You don't need to see what's coming."

Lucy gulped as she looked into his hazel eyes. They were laced with genuine concern. "It's that certain?"

"We've convicted with far less before," he said as he shook his head. "Trust me—you don't want to see this."

Lucy couldn't help but look up at the front of the court

where Eddie's proud posture slumped as the judge read out the guilty verdict. "You are hereby sentenced to death by firing squad, effective immediately."

"How immediate?" she croaked out as Eddie scanned the audience for help and support and found only her. Lucy wasn't sure, but there seemed to be silent pleading in his eyes followed by a flash of anger. Was that also hurt and betrayal that she saw in his gaze? She just wasn't sure. She realized she didn't know who her brother was anymore.

The back doors of the courtroom opened, and four Jaegers in full battle armor marched in. Their brass armor clanked and they held beamer rifles at the ready as they walked past Lucy and Gabriel on their way to the front, tinted faceplates hiding all facial features.

"Very. Immediate," Gabriel said, now pulling on her arm. He got her standing and led her out the back. Lucy felt like she was in a daze as Gabriel pulled her along. Just as the doors closed, she heard the crack of four beamer rifles firing in perfect precision.

"Oh, God," she breathed as she fainted into Gabriel's arms.

***

Lucy was let out of the steam carriage's back compartment when Gabriel opened the door for her. After she'd come to, he helped her outside to a public carriage that was waiting to take her home after it was confirmed that her brother was indeed dead. She squeezed his hand as she stepped out.

"Thank you, Mr. McKibben, for everything."

"Yeah," he said in a hollow voice and then looked toward the front door of her estate. "Would you like me to come in? I can break the news to your parents if you'd like?"

She shook her head. "No, thank you. They should probably hear it from me."

"Look," Gabriel said, and fished a card from his uniform pocket. "If you need anything, call me. You can get a hold of me though any Consortium office should you lose that. Just ask for me by my callsign," he said as he gave the card to her.

"Jaeger Messenger." Lucy looked at the card and gave

him a wan smile. "Why Messenger?"

"A wicked messenger falls into adversity while a faithful one brings healing," he quoted with a proud upward flourish of his hand as if delivering a soliloquy. "Proverbs, in the One Book."

Lucy regarded him in a new light. "I didn't figure you for one who followed scripture."

"Well, I sure as hell didn't get my callsign from sending letters in the mail system," Gabriel said with a shrug. "Theocracy habits die hard, I guess."

"Will I get to see you again?"

He answered her with a smile, took her hand in his, and brushed his lips to her knuckles.

"Have as good of an evening that you can, Lady Spence," he replied before hopping back into the carriage and thumping on the side to get the driver moving.

Lucy watched the carriage chug off before absently bringing her hand up to her face. She was sure that it was her imagination, but it really felt as though she could feel the warmth of his touch lingering on her skin. Letting out a wistful sigh along with a pang of regret for what could have been, Lucy turned and entered her mansion.

The first thing that she noticed was that the serving staff was conspicuously missing. In their place was a legion of clockworks, all moving with purpose from room to room as they packed things and transferred belongings around.

"What on earth?" she muttered as she moved from the entry hall farther into the building. She stopped a clockwork. "Where are Mother and Father?"

It pointed her in the direction of the drawing room before moving off to complete its assigned task. With mounting trepidation, Lucy walked into the drawing room to find her mother in tears while she packed mementos away into an oversized carpet bag, and her father, stern as ever, staring out the window with hands clasped behind his back.

"Mother?" Lucy asked cautiously. "Father? What... what's going on?"

"Our marriage has been dissolved," Reverend Edward Spence the Second said gruffly without turning around.

Lucy's hand went to her chest as she gasped and reached

25

for the nearest chair before her legs gave out. Her father was a big barrel of a man whose looks many often compared to the old American president, Theodore Roosevelt.

"Dissolved?" Lucy squeaked. "How can that be?"

It was her mother, Jennifer, who answered in a hollow voice. "After learning what went on at the trial from one of his associates, your grandfather decreed that, in the wake of this scandal, I return home to the family estate with my children while the Spences are under further investigation by both the Consortium and now the Theocracy."

Her eyes came up to meet her eldest daughter's, and Lucy was taken aback to see a flash of anger and hatred in them. *They blame me*, Lucy thought, as an overwhelming glumness came over her.

"We have to leave home?" Lucy asked as she pictured her whole world start to shatter. "But... but this is where I grew up and... and I'm to be formally declared at the gala this September."

"No," Jennifer shook her head. "I said me and *my* children. Eddie is gone, thanks to *you,* and I have no first-borne daughter anymore thanks to *my* father saying as such."

Lucy was bombarded with a wave of grief at her mother's rejection.

"I am taking Eve and Amanda with me. *You* will be staying here...." Her mother's eyes flicked over toward Edward. "That assumes your father sees fit to keep you."

"You don't have worry about your betrothed, either," Edward replied in a subdued tone. "He pulled out of the arrangement. While you've been preoccupied with that Jaeger and the trial for the past week, rumors have come out that you've been, let us say, less than pure in your ways."

"What?" Lucy could scarcely believe what she was hearing. Ladd *had* been telling the truth in that she was being cut off. "But, that is preposterous! I've been staying at the hotel the Consortium provided while the trial was in progress!"

"Yes... I believe 'protective custody' was the term that they gave us. At any rate, your fiancé, or should I say former fiancé, says that the prospect of marrying you now is far too risky and the bride price is much too high now." He turned and glared at her in the way that she was all too familiar with.

26

It was the look she received whenever she was in serious trouble.

Lucy felt herself start to hyperventilate under her parents' hard gazes and coldness. Disowned by her maternal family and disavowed by the man she'd been promised to, all at once! On the very day her brother died, no less! Her head started to spin as she tried to wrap her mind around what was happening. One question came to mind.

"Why?" she asked as tears welled up. "Why am I being punished? Why are you all acting like this is *my* fault?

Jennifer started to speak, but Edward silenced her with a sharp upraised hand. "Because it was your testimony that helped doom your brother. Without it, he might still be living!" he snapped, his face turning red with anger.

"Would you have rather *I* went to prison... or worse?" Lucy was aghast. "I called you for help, Father, and you are acting like I was in league with Eddie's scheme to destroy the Carmichaels!"

Now it was Lucy who pointed an accusing finger at him as she gained some of her nerve. At this point, she didn't have much else to lose. In fact, she didn't have anything to lose. "You left me at the Consortium office all alone and it took a Jaeger to get me the message that I'd be on my own." She couldn't help but gape at them now. "We used to be such good friends with the Carmichaels. What happened?"

"What happened was that you were too frivolous in your spending and that tipped the Carmichaels off," her father growled. "Who, in turn, tipped the Jaegers off. So yes, this is all your fault."

"But...." Lucy's voice trailed off. "But, I was only doing what Eddie instructed me to do to begin with, which I assumed...." Her voice trailed off again as a realization dawned on her, "which I assumed came from you, Father."

"We were that close to getting the Carmichael-Bell Aircraft Plants, too," he grumbled. His trailing gaze sharpened on his daughter again. "And you are forbidden to tell anyone I said that or, so help me, I will have the constables end you!" He waved a dismissive hand. "Now get out of my sight before I have half a mind to sell you off to one of our few remaining allies.

Seeing no other choice, Lucy fled the room in tears.

CHAPTER 4

In an upscale lounge in the heart of Atlanta, Lucy stared morosely at the amber liquid in her wine glass. She'd long lost count of how many glasses she'd had this evening, but she'd stopped caring long ago. Even the revelry that was going on around her in celebration of Consortium Day couldn't lift her spirits.

Her mother was gone to grandfather's house along with her sisters, and her own father had stopped speaking to her. It was only a matter of time until she'd be forced to leave, assuming her father would decide that. So, she'd made the decision for him and took what remained of her own money to move into a modest apartment in the city.

What really troubled her was the fact that she had no idea what to do with her life now. She needed to do something, as her meager savings would not last long. A source of income was desperately needed. Until now, her life had been mapped out and thoroughly planned for her by her father and older brother. She had been a good girl, following all rules and directives laid out for her, but in the end, that was not enough. Lucy faced a grim reality that she'd be ejected out of the aristocracy, the only life she'd ever known. She stared long into her wine, searching for some vision of things to come. Fear gripped her as she realized that she had no real skills in which to garner employment anywhere.

Fully engrossed in her own self-pity, Lucy had long since drowned out the dimly lit parlor room, the chatting guest in their plush seats having a grand old time, and even the band on stage playing soft contemporary music that beckoned couples to dance. Instead, she sat at the bar with her back to the parlor debating on whether or not to take another drink.

Before she could, a man's hand reached out and plucked the thin-stemmed wine glass from her grasp. "I think that you've had enough the way you're sitting there," he said.

Lucy looked up feeling fury at the man's audacity. Now was not the time to mess with her. Her sharp rebuke died immediately when she caught glimpse of the immaculate Jaeger uniform and the sad smile of the man wearing it.

"Gabriel," she exclaimed and then caught herself. "I-I mean, Jaeger Messenger! Sorry... um... it's good to see you," she stammered out as she recovered. Her hands flew around as she subconsciously checked her appearance to make sure everything was still in order and that she didn't look as disheveled as she felt.

"It's good to be seen," he said before nodding to the bar chair next to her. "May I?"

"Please," she said, gesturing to it in turn by way of invitation. "What brings you here tonight?"

"I reward myself with a bit of guilty vice every Friday evening," he said, looking at the glass that he'd taken from her. "And it seems like you have, as well. At least you're still upright with only a slight wobble." He held out a hand to steady her when she swayed a bit in her seat.

She felt annoyed by the perceived verbal jab at her indulgence. "What's the problem with that?"

Gabriel held up his hands in defense. "No problem, just an observation. That's all. I usually don't see single ladies in here all that often, nor do I ever recall you drinking this much." He took a sip from Lucy's glass, grimaced at the taste, and ordered his drink of choice from the bartender who'd migrated back down their way. The bartender gave a slight bow and hustled off to fill the order while Gabriel turned back toward Lucy. "And aren't you supposed to be escorted while going out in public?"

"Like that's done me a lot of good," Lucy said with a heavy sigh. She then updated him on the current happenings in her life, watching as he winced at the implication of her impending ejection from the upper class.

Gabriel playfully feigned hurt. "Oh, dear God, you poor thing. You might have to actually row in the cargo hold with the rest of us galley slaves." He gave her a lopsided grin.

Lucy narrowed her eyes and glared at him. "Don't judge me! You have no right... you left me!"

A brief flash of anger crossed Gabriel's face before it set to stone. "You had two choices—sit around and lament about it, or go out and do something. I chose the latter."

"So you became a Jaeger?"

"Eventually," Gabriel said. "Hopped the first airship I

could down to Elysium and joined the Consortium. That's when I volunteered for duty in the Theocracy so that I could protect others from befalling the same fate as my family had."

There was a twinge of bitterness in his voice. "Why do you live here, Mr. McKibben?" Lucy asked, studying him with growing intrigue. "You don't follow our ways and you seem to hold our government in contempt."

"I don't live here anymore... technically," Gabriel corrected, taking a quick drink of his beer as soon as the bartender set it down. "I still live down in Elysium. I'm merely assigned here as my area of operation." He let out a rueful chuckle. "Do you know that North America has more Jaegers assigned to it than anywhere else save for maybe Asia... and that's just because of sheer continental landmass. And out of that, we have more Jaegers in the Theocracy and the Wastelands than anywhere else."

This was new information for Lucy. "I've heard stories that Africa is worse off," she added defensively.

"One would think so, wouldn't they?" Gabriel said. "But, since the Consortium stepped in and started regulating things—especially slavery—the minor warlords, kingdoms, fiefdoms, and anything else that could be considered an organized country quickly stepped into line and got with the program. They're actually better off now than they have been in years."

Lucy eyed him. "Why did the Consortium legalize slavery across the world?"

Gabriel snorted, nearly inhaling his beer. "Are you serious? Even here, now, on Consortium Day, you have no idea why the Consortium came to be?"

She shook her head and he sighed.

"I'm beginning to wonder if the Consortium needs to take over education next," Gabriel said as he placed his drink on the bar. "During the Great War, after it had raged on for ten years, governments finally broke down and failed all over the world. For example, the former United States disintegrated into eight factions—the Corporations, Dixie, Texas, Sonora, California, Olympia, Dakota, and Coronado."

"I haven't heard of those last two countries." Lucy frowned, groggily trying to remember her geography.

30

"That's because they no longer exist. Today, we know Dakota and Coronado as its more combined common name—the Wastelands," Gabriel said morosely. "They held the majority of the food supply for the old United States and so were valuable targets until the very liberal use of thermal weapons reduced everything to cinders from the former state of Arkansas all the way northwest to the old Montana-Canadian border. Nowadays it's the huge desert that we all know and despise today."

"I see," Lucy said, wondering exactly where this conversation was going.

"Anyway," Gabriel continued, "Things like that went on all around the world and people used different reasons to justify imprisoning and enslaving others. The most common reason being religion, of course, since there are a lot of people out there who apparently justify it. Your own One Book, for example."

"It does not!" Lucy protested, taken aback by the implycation.

Gabriel rolled his eyes. "Oh, please. How many times have I heard that? Read anything from Genesis to Judges and you'll find the rules governing them and situations justifying them as good, wholesome, and favorable to thy Lord." He pressed his hands together in mock piety. "Since you all regard that book as the end all, be all, for your government, did you know that your father could just simply sell you off? Oh, wait, he already did in the form of your arranged marriage which was then called off when you said that he came in and took back a large sum of money from your father."

Lucy opened her mouth to protest, but her counter argument died on her lips as the sudden reality came crashing into her mind. He was right. Her now ex-fiancé had gone to her father and demanded the bride price back before declaring their impending nuptials to be over.

"Yup." Gabriel nodded at her. "Religion was the basis for much of the slavery that was going on in the world. So, us Jaegers stepped in to allow people to liberate as many as possible who had been forced into slavery. When we realized just what an impossible task that would be, the Consortium

31

then saw to it that slavery must be regulated as fairly as possible and that slaves be treated humanely by all the nations of the world. We determined the ground rules so that people would at least be treated decently and given the basic right to choose their fates... unlike the old days where you could shoot a slave between the eyes and not even get a slap on the wrist."

"I don't know why anyone would *choose* to be a slave," she muttered.

Gabriel shrugged. "Depends on the situation. The former slave in your house, Esmond, had a leather collar. Unfortunately for him, he went along with the conspiracy to try forcing the Carmichaels into slavery, which is illegal under Consortium law. So, now his collar is iron instead of leather or lace. Regardless, from what we learned from him during the trial, he went into voluntary slave status initially to pay off some sizable gambling debts to the Carmichaels before his contract was bought out by your family."

Lucy shook her head, unable to fathom what had driven Esmond to such lengths. Then she remembered something. "Charity Carmichael is a vSlave now, too. She's owned by that accountant who busted in with Deliverer."

"Ah, yes, Lucas Wolverton." Gabriel nodded. "From what we heard of their testimonies, she went into voluntary slavery with him for protection. Since your brother was making it look like she was draining the accounts, Theocracy law would have allowed him to force her and her family into servitude under him while he took control of their assets, including their airship and aircraft manufacturing facilities in Marietta." He then thought it over. "Probably could've scored Bertram Carmichael's seat on the security council in the process, as well. Either way, it's still paramount to forced slavery in the Consortium's book."

"Eddie...." Lucy was still shaking her head. "Why? Why did you try and do that?" she asked as if her dead brother could somehow answer her. No, that was stupid of her. She knew the reason. Her father had said as much. What pissed him off the most was that Eddie was caught doing it. But, she really didn't want to think about that right now. What she really wanted to think about was Gabriel's body being in such close proximity to hers. In fact, it was distracting her from the conversation. She decided to change the subject. "So, how are you celebrating this Consortium Day, Mr. McKibben?"

"Good food, good drink, and good company," he said with a small salute of his glass her way. "And, please—it's Gabriel."

"I could kiss you, Mr. McKibben... er... uh...." Her voice faltered and she blushed slightly. "Gabriel," she amended with a smile.

Gabriel gave her a roguish grin. "What's stopping you, then?"

He was right. What *was* stopping her? She was no longer betrothed and without a male family member to sponsor her. She couldn't enter the autumn courting season after the gala. Lucy was now essentially a free, single woman who could choose her own destiny.

That thought, in of itself, made her feel empowered. She could act on her own, see whom she wanted, and right now there was a fine specimen of a man in front of her. He had once been interested in her. Perhaps a part of him still was. Maybe it was the alcohol that she'd consumed, or maybe it that she simply didn't care anymore, but she found herself closing her eyes and leaning i toward him with her lips puckered. She missed his lips and bumped into his chin. Jerking back with wide eyes, she was afraid that he'd be angry for her faux pas, but then she melted when he just laughed it off.

"Shall I?" he asked with a charming smile as he leaned in.

"Mm, yes, please," she agreed, and puckered up again.

Gabriel's touch was soft as he slid a hand over her shoulder and behind her neck to draw her in. His lips were equally soft and warm as they brushed against hers. She felt elated, giddy, and naughty all at the same time.

"I have a room upstairs now," Lucy said, letting the alcohol throw her inhibitions to the wind. "I bought it with my own money, as I'm in the process of moving out of my father's house since he doesn't want me anyway."

"Well, that escalated quickly," Gabriel commented with a smirk.

Lucy threw her hands out wide in a 'who cares' gesture. "What can any member of my family do to me? They've already thrown me out."

***

Lucy woke up the next morning with a throbbing headache. As she came to, she realized that it wasn't just her head that was pounding, it was also the door to her apartment. Gathering the sheets around her body, she realized that she wasn't wearing anything more than her negligee and her petticoat. She held up a hand to her temple to dull the pain. "Okay!" she finally yelled out toward the door in the entryway. "Please, be still! I just woke up!"

She looked around, confused. Gabriel was nowhere to be found. Frowning, her gaze settled on his card on the bedside table. She picked it up and saw that he'd written a note on the back.

You were drunk last night and I couldn't take advantage of that. So, I put you to bed. Call me when you have a clear head and we can try again. Gabriel.

"Oh, Gabriel," she sighed as she smiled, feeling warm inside. She then wondered just what she had said to him last night. The evening's events were quite fuzzy to her in the daylight hours.

The pounding at the door started up again and Lucy rolled her eyes and sighed. Whoever it was just would not go away. She donned a robe that was hanging over the edge of her fainting couch and cinched it tight as she walked to the door. Maybe it was Gabriel coming back. Had he spent the night? She put a bright smile on her face as she opened the door.

"Yes?"

Only it wasn't Gabriel. Four Theocracy constables stood there with serious looks on their faces. "Miss Lucy Spence?" one constable asked. Lucy noticed the stripes on his bicep and determined him to be a sergeant.

She lifted her chin with dignity as her smile faded. "*Baroness* Spence, if you please," she said with flash of fire in her eyes. "Or, at the very least, Lady. I still have that much, at

34

least... despite what my father says."

The sergeant shook his head. "Not anymore. You are under arrest for violation of the basic tenants of Theocracy society as outlined in First Timothy and are scheduled for trial early tomorrow morning." He motioned to one of his men, who reached out and grabbed her by the upper arm to pull her out of the doorway.

"How dare you touch me!" Lucy cried out, shaking off the man's grip. She backed up as the constables crowded in. "What is the charge?"

The arresting constable had a grave look as he fished his wrist shackles out from his back pocket. "For bearing false witness against an elder male of your family that led to his murder by the Consortium."

CHAPTER 5

Lucy was arrested and arraigned in a matter of hours. She knew that the justice system in this day and age was an expeditious process, but this seemed blindingly fast. Events were unfolding faster than she could process them. She was grateful that at least the constables had allowed her to dress properly into a corset and dress instead of being hauled in wearing nothing more than her petticoats

She spent the morning trying to get an advocate for the proceedings. She made all the calls that she could and was repeatedly told that there were no Theocracy advocates available to represent her. She'd tried contacting Gabriel through the Consortium, but they couldn't find him, and told her that he had the day off and they would try him at home. What was worse was that her own father said nothing and hung up the phone on her!

She had been wondering where her father's advocate was until she saw him sitting across the way at the prosecution table early the next morning. Her eyes went wide when Mr. Ladd gave her an evil, knowing wink and a smile as the bailiff cited some reference out of the One Book that she only caught part of after he'd read out the case and charges.

"Mr. Ladd, what are you doing over there?" she gasped, as she was led to the defendant's table.

"My new job, young lady, in trying my first case as a prosecutor for the Theocracy," he said, taking on an air of confidence. "I left your father's employ after your brother's trial with the Consortium. A trial, I might add, that has permanently marred my perfect win record thanks to your family. Now today I will see justice done by rectifying the mistake that the Consortium has made by letting you go loose!"

Lucy was stunned as she realized the reason for his absurd lines of questioning at Eddie's trial when she testified. He was just setting himself up for a sure-fire win to get back at her! She knew how good he was and her heart sank into the deepest pit of her stomach. Without an advocate to represent her, she would have to represent herself and there was no way that she could win with that... that snake!

"All rise!" the court bailiff announced. "This court is now in session. The Honorable Bartholomew Takacy presiding!"

Lucy's eyes widened as she stood on shaky legs. She had to use the desk for support. She knew that Judge 'Takacy the Terror' from the Kentucky Province was one of the worst judges to draw for a trial. The man had a reputation all over the continent for being one of the most ruthless judges around. He struck terror into the hearts and minds of defendants as he had a habit of always finding them guilty for one thing or another. Takacy offered the most insincere smile Lucy had ever seen.

"Good morning, y'all, you may be seated."

As everyone took their seats, Takacy looked over at Ladd and smiled, this time in a friendly manner. "Prosecutor, are you ready to proceed?" he asked in his deep Kentuckian drawl.

Lucy took and deep breath and sighed. She could not believe this was happening. And she was here, alone, without any help and support. She was doomed.

"I am, your Honor," Ladd said, standing up and nodding.

"Miss," Takacy then asked, looking at Lucy, "are you ready to proceed?"

"N-no, your... your Honor," Lucy said in a shaky voice. "I-I do not have an advocate." She indicated the empty chair and then looked around hopelessly for support. The courtroom was surprisingly barren of any witnesses except for a stony-faced man in the back with a smug look on his face. She recognized him from her brother's trial and wondered why he was here.

"Well, little lady, you should've thought about that before you got here," Takacy said, drawing her attention back. "Let's begin. Miss, you will take the accused's dais. Prosecutor, call yer first witness."

Before Ladd could say anything, the double doors at the back of the courtroom burst open, causing everyone to turn. Lucy's heart leapt when she saw Gabriel striding in, donning his formal Jaeger dress uniform as he carried a briefcase under his arm. "I apologize for being late, your Honor. My

37

office just contacted me about these proceedings. I will be acting as the advocate for the accused," he said hastily, as he removed his beret and slid over into the seat next to Lucy, pulling her back down to sit. He set the case down and opened it. Quills and parchment sprang up for his notetaking. He grabbed up the arraignment papers that were on the table in front of Lucy and started flipping through them as quickly as possible.

"What are you doing here?" Lucy leaned in and asked in a whisper. "Not that I'm ungrateful, mind you."

"I didn't get your message until a runner got to my apartment. I wasn't expecting to work today. When I got to the office, where it's causing quite the stir, I got the full details. Your arrest is all over the place. Everyone at the Consortium regional office is up in arms, but they won't be able to do anything right this second, so I came over as soon as I could to do what I can," Gabriel hastily explained before looking back at Takacy. "Your Honor, I move for an immediate continuance as I have not had time to go over the case with my client yet."

"Motion for a continuance denied, advocate. You should've gotten here sooner," Takacy said gruffly.

Gabriel looked dumbfounded as he rocked back in his seat. This did not help Lucy's confidence.

"Can I at least get a quick recess?" he asked.

"Your Honor," Ladd piped up, pointing at Gabriel. "I object to a Jaeger being here in these proceedings. He has no legal standing here and this is a Theocracy matter—not a Consortium matter."

"As well you should since you know I'll mop the floor with you again," Gabriel growled at him. He then looked at the judge. "I am licensed for advocacy in the Theocracy of Dixie, the Corporate States of America, the Island Confederation of Elysium, and the City-State of Vegaston, your Honor, with certifications pending in Sonora and the Californian Republic." Gabriel opened his briefcase and produced several papers. He held them up for both Takacy and Ladd to see. "I can produce all of my licenses and BAR certifications for your review." He gave them to the clerk who then handed them to the judge.

Takacy's clenched jaw worked while he scanned the documents. Gabriel leaned in toward Lucy.

"I believe he had been about to uphold the objection and bounce me out of here, but he's not going to be able to now," he whispered.

"The court accepts you as advocate for the defense," Takacy said through gritted teeth. "But, you watch your tone in my court, boy, or I will hold you in contempt—Jaeger or not."

Gabriel fished out a gold coin from his pocket and flipped it up to the judge. "Fuck you," he said defiantly. He then grabbed another and flipped it up to him as well. "And while I'm at it, buy yourself a hairpiece. Your gray comb-over looks hideous." Gabriel looked at Ladd. "Get on with it."

"Are you insane?" Lucy asked in a hushed voice when he sat back down. "You just insulted the judge. He can have you arrested!"

"Not on contempt of court. It's merely a single gold fine per offense. So long as I have gold to toss at him, I can insult him all I want to." Gabriel grinned at her. "Relax, I've called Theocratic judges far worse and gotten away with it."

Up at the bench, Takacy glared daggers at them, but turned his attention back to Ladd. "You may proceed with your opening arguments, prosecutor."

"Thank you, your Honor," Ladd said and stepped from behind his desk and went up to the witness dais. "This is a very simple case and the facts speak for themselves. Recently, Miss Lucy Spence did, of her own accord, bear false witness against her own brother, then Baron Edward Spence the Third. This witnessing and testimony resulted in the downfall of a once prominent house within our great country and has set an unprecedented standard in which doors are now open to allow women to rise up against their proper male masters."

"What?" Gabriel whispered to himself and then leaned in to Lucy while Ladd droned on and on. "What have you been charged with, exactly?" he asked, looking through the papers again for the arrest details.

Lucy sighed, and her eyes began to burn. It was taking all her strength not to burst into tears. "Murder of my brother, bearing false witness, and inciting dissention among the female populace of the country."

"Are you fucking serious? They're blaming you for Eddie's death? He was convicted by the Consortium, not the Theocracy. This is insane!" Gabriel looked up at the judge. "Objection, your Honor," he said, shooting to his feet, and interrupting Ladd who was in the middle of his opening argument. "Edward Spence the Third was found guilty in a Consortium court."

"We're in opening arguments, Jaeger!"

"And neither of us have been given the opportunity to present initial motions prior, your Honor," Gabriel countered. "We shouldn't even be having this trial!"

"Objection overruled. Prosecutor, please continue," Takacy said amid Gabriel's perplexed look.

"Thank you," Ladd said, inclining his head toward the judge as Gabriel sat down, glowering. "As I was saying, it was one of the greatest leaders of our precursor nation who stated that a house divided against itself could not possibly stand."

"He also said that the religion allows humans to act inherently selfish, too, but I don't hear you quoting *that* one," Gabriel muttered loud enough for just Lucy to hear.

Lucy couldn't help but smile.

Ladd continued, oblivious to Gabriel's comment. "Indeed, that is what has happened here. A woman of the once noble Spence household, against the express orders of her father and her dearly departed older brother, divided her house. I will prove, beyond any doubt, that Miss Spence singlehandedly orchestrated the downfall of her entire house and will therefore encourage others to do the same, throwing our beloved country that has stood tall for well over a hundred years."

"Technically only seventy-five. You don't get to count the Confederate States of America or the time under the United States, idiot," Gabriel grumbled.

Takacy shifted his gaze over to Gabriel. Where he'd been smiling at Ladd, he frowned at Gabriel. "Get on with your opening arguments, advocate."

***

Taking a deep breath, Gabriel stood up, but not before giving Lucy a reassuring pat on her folded hands. "Hang in there—this is gonna be rough."

He stood, tugging down on his uniform tunic to straighten it, squared his shoulders, and walked out in front of the defendant's table.

"Your Honor, the charges against my client are not only false, but they are taking an otherwise innocent and innocuous law and blowing it way out of context," he said as a preamble.

He glanced over at Ladd. *You wanna cite history, little man, alright... let's play.*

"Well over eighty years ago, when the nations of our world dissolved, there were little rights for anyone. It was the Consortium that stepped in to bring law and order to chaos. It was the Consortium that ensured that a level playing field was available to all."

He looked Takacy square in the eye as he came up with his opening argument on the fly. "Baroness Lucy Spence did not murder her brother. Her brother, the late Edward Spence the Third, died of his own accord when he violated the Consortium's basic right of choice. He was lawfully executed by the Consortium when his crimes came to light." Gabriel pointed at Lucy. "Mr. Spence used his own sister to unknowingly carry out these crimes, which is why the Consortium found her to be not guilty of collusion with her brother. The sins of the father do not translate down to be the sins of the son, and in this case, the sins of the brother do not translate over as punishment to the sister."

Shaking his head for emphasis, Gabriel spread his hands in askance. "Women of the Theocracy do not have many rights, and one of their primary directives is to obey higher authority. This was the case with my client; she was obeying the highest authority of the land. She rendered unto Caesar that which was Caesar's and did the only thing that she could've done in such a situation—she testified against her brother for the Consortium. The Consortium found her innocent, and you should, too."

41

Turning sharply on his heel, Gabriel went back to his seat.

Lucy was already leaning in to him to speak. "That was impressive."

"I'm just getting warmed up, sweetheart." He grinned at her.

Up on the bench, Takacy's jaw was visibly clenching as he glared at Gabriel. Then his gaze shifted to Ladd. "Call yer first witness."

Ladd slowly stood. "The Theocracy calls Miss Lucy Spence, your Honor."

"Objection!" Gabriel shot to his feet, outraged. "The Fifth Right of the Consortium forbids testimony against oneself regardless of nationality. My client does not waive that right."

Ladd gave a pleading look toward Takacy. "Your Honor, this is a Theocracy matter."

"So you keep saying," Gabriel glowered at him. "It doesn't allow you to circumvent Consortium Law. Call someone else."

"Objection is sustained," Takacy ground out between clenched teeth. "Move on."

Ladd did so, and spent the next half hour presenting evidence that was mainly references to past cases before culminating with Eddie Spence's own case. The final piece of evidence was a local minister who droned on about the virtues of the Theocracy and how their way of life was superior before citing more references from the One Book. By the time Ladd was finished, Gabriel felt like he was going to fall asleep. He didn't even bother to redirect.

Ladd looked at Gabriel with a look of triumph. "The Theocracy rests."

Gabriel stood up. "The defense would like to enter in motions before proceeding."

"It doesn't matter. I've come to my decision," Takacy interrupted.

"What? That's it? Are you serious?" Gabriel thundered, aghast at how much of a show trial this had been. He couldn't help looking at the gear clock off to the left. He'd barely been in the courtroom for an hour! "Just like that? Right after calling just one witness and citing a bunch of bullshit?" he asked Takacy, his anger swelling. "I get no evidence, no questioning, no deliberations, no arguments, no moving to a jury, nothing?"

Trials moved fast in the Theocracy, but this one moved faster than a Tesla engine on overdrive. He'd been practicing law in this country for years, and this was the first time that a trial was over before it'd even begun. So much for due process.

"I have no need for deliberations or anything of the sort as this matter is already settled," Takacy said with a cruel smile and an air of arrogance. "Miss Spence, this court finds you guilty as charged."

CHAPTER 6

Gabriel knew where this was going. It was like watching two massive airships collide in slow motion. Over in her seat, Lucy looked pale and faint. Nothing that he said or did was going to change the court's mind. He pulled Lucy down from the dais, draped his arm over her shoulders so that he could lean in close as he led her back to her seat. "Opt for iSlave status. Now!" he hissed quietly and urgently as they sat.

"Are you mad?" Lucy asked him. "I will *not* be sold off at public auction!"

"You'd rather go to a breeder farm?" Gabriel growled, gesturing angrily at the judge. "Because I guarantee that's where you're going to be sentenced to in about five seconds! Look, we're *way* past keeping you out of prison, and now all I can do is mitigate damages." His eyes silently pleaded with hers as he spoke quickly. "At least as an iSlave, you still have some options about where you end up. But, if you remain an inmate, you are completely at his mercy!" he pointed at Takacy for emphasis. "Opt for it. Now!"

Wide-eyed as the implication hit her, Lucy shot back to her feet before Takacy could pass sentencing. He was in the process of conferring with Ladd about what a "proper" sentence would be. Gabriel could hear the words like 'whoresville' and other euphemisms for the breeder prison camps for women, and knew Lucy could, too.

"Y-your Honor! I wish to enter into involuntary slavery status as guaranteed by the Consortium!" she cried out, her voice shaky.

Takacy and Ladd paused their conversation before slowly turning to look at Lucy. They both gaped at her before Takacy was the first to recover.

"I'm sorry, little lady, but that just ain't happening," he said, his insincere smile returning. "You are hereby sentenced to the Taylorsville Penitentiary for Women for a period of no less than ten years, remanded into the custody of Overseer Clark Anderson who is standing by for you," he said and nodded toward the expressionless man at the back of the court.

"Objection, your Honor," Gabriel shouted as he rose to his feet in an attempt to move fast before Takacy could bring down his gavel, and finalize this horrific sentence. "No person found guilty of a crime may be denied consideration for involuntary slavery status in lieu of sentencing unless that crime is capital in nature and the accused has been found to be a physical danger to society!" He gestured to Lucy. "Miss Spence is *not* a violent offender and the crime that *this so-called court* has found her guilty of is not violent in nature. Therefore, my client poses no risk to the general populace, and cannot be denied iSlave status under Consortium law!"

"That might be true in a Consortium court, Jaeger," Takacy said disdainfully, "but here in the Theocracy, only men are allowed that right. As First Timothy, Chapter Two, states in the One Book, she should learn about quietness and submissiveness for Adam was formed first and was not deceived."

"Leviticus Nineteen, Verse Fifteen," Gabriel countered, snapping the citation out just as quickly. "Do not pervert justice, but judge your neighbor fairly." He glared right at the judge. "The Consortium regulates the control, rules, and regulations regarding the disposition of *all* slaves and inmates, regardless of nationality, and therefore you cannot overrule a basic right to choose given to *all* people of the world. I move that my client be remanded into my custody to undergo processing as an involuntary slave."

"Your motion is denied, Jaeger," Takacy shot back, "and I am not in a habit of being questioned in my own courtroom. Deuteronomy Chapter Sixteen, Verse Eighteen: Appoint judges and officials for each of your tribes in every town the Lord—your God—is giving you."

"How about you keep on quoting that verse since it ends in 'and they shall judge the people fairly,' huh?" Gabriel snapped. "Then let's polish it off with the Cow, Chapter Two, Verse Forty-Two: Confound not the truth with falsehood, nor knowingly conceal the truth. The truth of the matter being that despite a conviction my client *still* has the basic right to opt for that status!"

"I see why they call you the Messenger," Lucy whispered. "Can you recite every verse of the book and use them to help your arguments?" she said with a wink.

Gabriel smiled at Lucy, happy to have impressed her. Takacy, however, was unfazed,

"We must remember what Our Savior would have us do in such a situation," he said, adopting the tone of a preacher.

"Yeah?" Gabriel snorted, "well, flipping tables and chasing people with a bullwhip isn't outside the realm of possibility on that one. If you'd like, I can start that now for my opening act and end with an official investigation as to why *you* are denying someone a very basic right of choice, as guaranteed by the Consortium, regardless of nationality, theology, or ideology. Now what is it going to be? I haven't even gone into the fact that you already have an overseer here to take custody which, to me, suggests that you came to a *predetermined* verdict without proper due process!" He paused to let the implication of a kangaroo court or a show trial set in as he locked eyes with Takacy. "Now, are you going to grant my client involuntary slave status as requested, or do I call up New Eden and have them send an auditing team and even more Jaegers up here to start looking into all of your court records?"

Takacy flinched at the threat and Ladd blanched. Gabriel inwardly sighed... he *finally* had them. He might not be able to keep Lucy from being sentenced right this second, but he could at least mitigate the punishment for her a bit. Why the hell did this judge have such a hard-on for sending such a petty offense to a breeder farm to which the overseer of said farm was already in attendance? That wasn't a normal proceeding as far as he knew. For that matter, why the hell was something as simple as bearing witness against her own brother being punished like this? He was determined to get the answers and ensure the proper justice for Lucy.

Takacy locked eyes with Gabriel, jaw twitching. Gabriel stared right back, silently daring the judge to say anything other than what he wanted to hear right now.

"Fine," Takacy finally snapped out. "Ten years as an involuntary slave to be sold off at public auction at the end of the week," he ground out, banging his gavel down. "Miss Spence, you're remanded into the custody of the *local* Consortium to await auction. Bailiff, take her away. Court is adjourned."

46

He banged his gavel down again to dismiss everyone and was up and out of there as fast as his chubby legs could carry him. In the back of the courtroom, the overseer in question shot to his own feet and strode out of the courtroom in obvious anger.

The grim-faced bailiff came from the side and took Lucy by her upper arm. She gave an alarmed, questioning look to Gabriel and made a whimpering noise. Gabriel swore under his breath at the Judge's wording in such a way that he couldn't take Lucy. He shook his head at her to indicate that she shouldn't do anything.

"Don't resist him. Go with him. I am going to get to the bottom of this and figure out if I can appeal. In the meantime, follow their instructions." Gabriel said.

Lucy swallowed hard and gave him a shaky nod before being led off. She looked devastated and frightened—rightfully so. He hated to see her dragged away like this.

"You have no grounds for appeal, Mr. 'Messenger.' Jaeger or no," Ladd said, now standing behind Gabriel. "This is a Theocracy matter."

Gabriel turned and gave him a hard stare that could rival beamer shots. "You *really* don't want to go down that line of thought with me right now," he said with so much ice in his voice that it threatened to drop the temperature in the room by a few degrees despite the hot summer day.

Ladd's eyes went wide and he backed up as Gabriel advanced on him, itching for a reason to arrest the man. "Enjoy your win for now, since I promise you that I'm going to be taking a keen interest in all of your cases from here on out."

With that, Gabriel gathered up his papers and his briefcase and stormed out of the room before he did something stupid, like fry a lawyer with his sidearm. Besides, he had some emergency calls to make. He just hoped that whoever oversaw Lucy's processing would go easy on her or else there'd be hell to pay.

***

With a constable holding her by her upper arms, Lucy was

marched to the gate of a holding cell where she was unceremoniously flung inside. She managed to keep her composure despite the lecherous grins on the constables' faces. One of them jerked his chin upwards toward her. "Strip."

Lucy blinked, unsure if she'd heard him correctly. "I beg your pardon?"

"You heard me," the constable said, his features hardening. "Strip so that we can thoroughly search you."

Her heart was pounding. First the conviction and now this! Was this what happened to all women who were found guilty of a crime? It was unthinkable!

"That won't be necessary, gentlemen," Lucy heard a man say in a pleasant, but firm tone. Lucy and the constable looked toward the door, where the voice had come from. She saw a man standing there in an immaculate three-piece suit holding up his Consortium credentials. He had a roguish grin that was easily visible underneath of his neatly trimmed black goatee.

"Coleton Muller, Consortium processing. This young lady comes with me."

The constable that had ordered Lucy to divest herself of her clothing gave Coleton a sly smile. "We have to process her first *before* we hand her over to you. That is procedure."

Coleton pocketed his identification and then pulled out a clipboard that was tucked under his arm and consulted it. He pulled the magnifying glasses from the top of his head down to his forehead so that he could make a show of studying the document in detail.

"Hmm, this is Miss Lucy Spence, just now convicted and who had opted for iSlave status, yes?" He pushed the glasses back up and gave them an insincere smile. "Procedures state that processing of iSlaves happens at the Consortium level. Of course, you'd know that if this particular courtroom handled more cases such as this one, but I am sure that fine, upstanding constables like yourselves will refresh your memories on proper proceedings if this happens in the future, yes?"

The constables' confident grins drooped as Coleton continued his spiel. He tucked the clipboard back under his arm and adopted a solemn posture.

"Gentlemen, I assure you that this matter will be taken care of properly in accordance with *Consortium* law." He lifted a hand to shoo them off. "Now, go on. I'm sure you have work to do and everything... like keeping the streets of Atlanta safe from ungodly heathens such as myself. Go on. Chop, chop, on your way now." He watched them with an expectant look as they cast forlorn glances Lucy's way and then trudged out of the holding area.

Reluctantly and cautiously, Lucy peeked her head out of the gate. Coleton smiled and beckoned her forward.

"You're safe now, Miss Spence." He offered the crook of his arm to her. "If you don't mind, we'll get you to the proper holding facility until auction."

"Umm... thank you," she said, her voice a little shaky, as she placed her arm inside his. "I dare say thank goodness for your prompt arrival. The trial had just ended."

"Yes," Muller agreed as he led her back out into the corridors behind the courtrooms. "Your trial has caused quite the stir. The local Consortium offices are all up in arms and believe me when I tell you that the Jaegers are throwing a fit."

"How did you get here so fast?"

Coleton let out a long breath. "As much as we hate to admit it, your conviction was a certainty. When Messenger rushed out of his office to be your advocate, I was dispatched to be your handler since there was no way he was going to win." He gave her an apologetic look. "Messenger is good, don't get me wrong, but I don't think even he could've convinced Takacy to rule in your favor."

"You know of him?"

"I think that you'd be hard-pressed to find someone in the Consortium who hasn't heard of him." Coleton grinned as he opened the door that led to an alley, where he helped her into the back of a steam car before following her. The moment the door was closed, the engine roared to life and they were off. "Judge Takacy has been on the Consortium's radar for some time now. In fact, some of the ladies that will be going up to auction are a result of his rulings this past week."

"So, there's nothing you or Gabriel can do?"

Coleton spread his hands in an apologetic gesture. "Just hang in there. I've never seen Messenger so impassioned about a case before. If anyone can find something that we can nail Takacy to the wall with, it'll be him. And, if I know Messenger, he's already filed motions to appeal."

***

Gabriel wanted to ram his head into the wall as he figured that he'd get better results that way. Instead, he snarled as he slammed the phone receiver down into its holder before running his hands through his hair. Another dead end.

"Gah!"

When he started his journey to become a Jaeger in the Theocracy, he knew that he'd be stonewalled by the legal system, but even this was ridiculous.

The moment he'd returned from the courtroom, he started making calls to everyone that he knew who could pull strings. He also filed his motions for an appeal. As it stood now, no one wanted to cross Judge Takacy. Before today, Gabriel had only heard of the man by reputation, and from what he'd seen, it was a well-deserved one.

Grabbing a couple of legal journals and Theocracy statutes from his bookshelf, he started flipping through them, seemingly at random, until he got to the references that he wanted. While studying the texts with a finger, he wrote notes on his parchments with his free hand.

For hours, he scoured documents and manuals on every legal option he could attempt. His studies were interrupted when the phone rang. Gabriel grabbed it, hoping it was a return call from an inquiry he'd made earlier. He needed answers, though he wasn't holding his breath for happy news.

"Messenger," he said, bracing himself.

"Good evening, Messenger, this is Clerk Jericho from Supreme Court of the Theocracy. I wanted to let you know that your, ah, request for an expedited appeal hearing has been denied and thus the original ruling of Judge Takacy will stand."

"Yah-huh...," Gabriel said dryly, feeling disappointed though not surprised.

50

"Furthermore," Jericho continued, confirming Gabriel's suspicions, "the Supreme Court will be filing a formal protest into your actions with the Consortium first thing in the morning. They are none too pleased that you infringed upon the legal proceedings of a Theocratic court."

"Right, thank you," Gabriel said curtly, placing the receiver down before flinging the phone across the room. The protest would go nowhere. Were he just a mere lawyer then the Consortium might have looked into it. Being a Jaeger, though, they'd give it all the consideration it was due, have a good laugh at it, and then probably congratulate him on shaking things up in the Theocracy.

He looked at his notes, crumpled them up, and tossed them into the wastebasket. Plans A, B, and C were toast. Now to go on to Plan D. Theocracy legal proceedings were done. It was time to escalate things to the Consortium.

**

Lucy fought to keep the tears from welling up in her eyes as she looked at her nude self in the mirror. Now that she'd been forced to undress, reality was setting in and it was more than she could bear. At least the Consortium officials had the decency to not gawk at her like those Theocracy goons had been doing. The Consortium guard looked at her with a touch of concern once she handed over her clothes.

"This might seem empty and hollow, but do try to relax. Everyone goes through this and you're far from the first. Now, the auction is tomorrow so there's not much time for anything elaborate. You're kinda getting in right at the deadline. A day later and you'd be in here for a month until the next auction."

Frustrated, Lucy couldn't hide her feelings. "Is there a point to this?" she snapped, the tears now starting to flow. She was tired of all of this and she couldn't help herself anymore.

"Right, sorry," the guard said with a nod. "The point is that you are still entitled to a last request before you lose citizenship status and are sold off. Since time is of the essence here, I need to know what would you like it to be so that we can honor it," he explained.

This caught Lucy off guard; she really didn't know what to think. Everything was happening so fast that it made her head spin. She was about to be sold as a pleasure slave to serve at a man's whims and she didn't even know what to do in that regard. She had never felt so helpless and useless in her entire life.

Her thoughts turned to Gabriel, the only man she'd really ever wanted to sleep with, and he'd turned her down when she was too tipsy to remember anything. Could they have had the chance to reconnect if she hadn't gotten sentenced to slavery?

Thinking of her ex-fiancé from an age ago made her heart hurt. What had happened between them to make him run off like he did? Was it something that she had or hadn't done? Her mind drifted and she remembered being shy, coy, and innocent with him. At one point in time, he did try to bed her as his right, but she'd resisted per Eddie's orders and Gabriel had backed off. He was a real gentleman.

Her eyes fell to the pile of her clothes that had yet to be removed by the guard. "Yes...," she said slowly. "May I have the garter from my garments, please?" she asked, pointing to her dress. "I want to give it to someone. And, am I allowed to have some... umm... private time with Jaeger Messenger so I can wear it for him?" *Again...* she mentally added.

The guard gave her a small, knowing smile. "I can arrange that for you."

CHAPTER 7

"What's going on?" Gabriel asked as he entered the holding cell area underneath the Atlanta Open Market. It was dim down here with the briefest flicker of electric lanterns every few cells being the only light to see by. "My secretary said that it was urgent."

"My apologies for such a short notice, Honored Jaeger," the Consortium guard said, motioning for him to follow down the rows of cells. "Auction is tomorrow and you are Miss Spence's last request. We have her in a conjugal cell at the end of the block here. This way."

"Ah," Gabriel said as he walked with the guard past the open cells that held the inmates who awaited their assignments as involuntary slaves. Gabriel couldn't imagine having to choose between that status or the brutal realities of prison where they are forced into labor or menial work for the duration of their sentences.

The inmates awaiting auction were already wearing their iron collars, welded into place around their necks and their contract numbers engraved onto them.

The last request was an old tradition reserved for those going into iSlave status. Typically, it was a favored meal, or the request to read a certain book, or even to take in the theater before they went up onto the auction block. It was the last request they could make as a free man or woman before they lost all their rights for the term of their sentence. The fact that Gabriel was Lucy's last request made him wonder what exactly she wanted.

The guard unhooked the heavy key ring from his belt and opened one of the two doors at the end of the cell block. "Here you are, sir," he said, opening the door like a butler. "You have until midnight, at which time I must come back and ask you to leave so that she can be cleaned and prepared for auction."

"Right," Gabriel said, patting the man on the shoulder. "Thank you," he said walking in.

The guard closed and locked the door behind him. The conjugal cell was larger than the typical cells he'd just passed and it was totally enclosed in brick with the heavy iron door being the only way in or out. There was a small enclosed shower along the wall that was shared with the other conjugal cell to Gabriel's right. Off to the left was a large, plush, four poster bed with white silks draped off the frame. It was lit by only the two electric lanterns that flanked the iron door behind him.

Lucy sat at the foot of the bed, naked save for her collar and a garter encircling her left thigh. She wrung her hands nervously.

"Hi," she said, looking down at her lap. "I guess you're wondering why you're here?"

"Yeah, I kinda am," he admitted even though he now had a good idea what she wanted. Seeing her completely nude before him was something that he'd pictured many times in his head in the past, but. reality blew fantasy away.

***

Lucy's heart was in her throat as she looked at Gabriel standing there.

She summoned the courage to look him in the eye. "I want to know why you didn't sleep with me that night when I practically threw myself at you?"

"Easy—you were drunk." Gabriel said with a disdainful snort. "I might be a skirt chaser on my days off, but I'm not a total lush. I took you up to your room, helped you out of your clothes without taking off your undergarments, and put you to bed. You actually passed out before you could plant another kiss on me." He smiled. "Not that the first one was bad, mind you."

Lucy smiled at him. She found him utterly charming. "Well, I'm not drunk now," she said and let out a rueful laugh. Tears brimmed in her eyes as she waved a callous hand toward the door. "They've already drawn up the paperwork for me. I'm going to be auctioned off as a...," her voice caught in her throat, "as a pleasure slave tomorrow."

"Aristocracy with no real domestic skills, yeah," Gabriel nodded grimly. "I imagine you'll go for a really high price, although not high enough to be the same as a bride price."

"I don't know how to do it!" Lucy blurted, which caused the awkwardness between them to rise slightly. She blushed and looked down again. "I'm still pure," she admitted. "I was... well... saving myself, but now...." Lucy stood up, squared her shoulders, and looked at him with tears streaming down her burning face. "I was hoping that you could be the one to take it."

***

Gabriel could feel conflicting emotions war against one another as he looked at her. The primal, chest beating, warrior-like part of his brain screamed for him to throw her onto the bed, take her in a manly fashion, and reclaim what had once been denied him. The gentleman part urged caution and warned him to take the moral high ground. His common sense reminded him that he'd be an idiot if he went through with this after everything that her family did to him and to others.

But, then there was a calming voice of reason reminding him that she had no part in her family's crimes. He'd determined that much in the line of her questioning and then again during her Theocracy show trial. He closed his eyes and took a deep, steadying breath to silence the conflicting voices. When he opened his eyes again, she was but a hair's breath away, looking expectantly up at him. He saw the innocent-looking girl that she once was, and the still-innocent woman who he'd rushed to defend on a whim.

"I shouldn't, Lucy...," he croaked out. "*We* shouldn't... I'm still acting on your behalf."

"Please. I want this, Gabriel... Gabe," Lucy said, pressing her naked breasts up against his uniform-clad chest as she rose onto her tiptoes, tilting her head back for an expectant kiss.

Oh, I'm going to roast in the special hell for this, Gabriel thought as their lips brushed one another. He felt the sensation of tiny electrodes fire from his lips to his groin as he embraced her and drew her close, kissing her deeply. Lucy moaned softly as she melted into his arms. The last bit of his resolve crumbled while his brain threw their proverbial hands in the air in defeat, and the primal portion of his being howled in victory.

With a hungry groan, Gabriel lifted Lucy and she wrapped her legs around his midsection as he carried her to the bed where he gently laid down, her hungry body beneath his. Their kissing grew frantic and urgent as they both knew that they had precious little time together.

Her hands grabbed at his jacket's immaculate brass buttons as he undid clasps of his uniform collar. The jacket was shucked off amid a tangle of moving arms, followed by the white long-sleeved undershirt. He freed his arms from his suspenders and then struggled to open his fly while their bodies ground together.

Once his cock sprang out, he slowed things down as much as he could handle. Her recently shaved pubis was already glistening, and he took the time to pause before he brought his cock up.

Gabriel broke from the passionate kissing long enough to look into her eyes. "Are you sure about this?" he asked.

Lucy spread her legs wide on the bed and reached down between them to wrap her hand around his hardness. "Take me," she whispered breathlessly into his ear as she guided him into position. "Please."

Gabriel moved his hips forward, slowly easing into her until the head of his cock met the resistance of her maidenhead. She winced and he let out a grunt as he pushed through. Lucy let out a muted cry into his shoulder. Then, the moment passed and they both relaxed as he slid into her all the way.

"Are you okay?" he asked, voice laced with genuine concern.

"Mm-hm..." she managed to nod. "Just... give me a moment?"

Gabriel nodded, running a hand through her blonde hair that was beginning to show streaks of her natural red color, while making soothing noises into her ear. Her chest heaved against his, and he could feel the tiny pinpricks of her nipples as they pressed and retreated from his skin with each breath that she took.

She indicated her readiness to continue when she

56

wrapped her legs back around his waist and her arms around his neck, drawing his body closer to hers. Gabriel sucked on the nape of her neck as he proceeded to move inside of her in slow, deliberate thrusts. Her winces of pain soon gave forth to moans of passion as her body accommodated his manhood within her. Soon, she was arching her back and lifting her hips to meet his thrusts.

"Oh!" she gasped when she felt his cock become even more engorged the moment before he came. His cock throbbed inside of her and he groaned hard and long as the passion overcame him. Once he was through, he lifted slightly to look down at her. She smiled back up at him.

"I hope that you enjoyed?" she asked sweetly.

"Uh... yeah... I think that'd be obvious," Gabriel replied, matching her smile. He lowered himself down to kiss her deeply. "I hope that you enjoyed it even a little bit."

"Definitely better than I thought it would be," Lucy admitted as he moved to one side to hold her. "I hope that you'll be able to do it again before you have to leave?"

Gabriel glanced over his shoulder at the clock on the wall. "Yeah," he nodded. "I should have at least one more in me, and the next time should be far more enjoyable." He then regarded her. "The way you grabbed me, I would've sworn you've done this before." *With other suitors who were not me....* He banished that painful idea. A shadow crossed her angelic features and Gabriel winced in his gaff.

"Well, some aristocratic families... pay... for their daughters to be appropriately trained before they're engaged, so that they can properly please their suitors," she said defensively.

"I'm sorry... I didn't think."

"No, it's okay. Really." She gave him a sideways look. "I figured you knew that since you're originally from the Theocracy."

"My family got cast out when I was young. Besides, us boys never knew what went on with you girls," Gabriel replied in a bitter tone, hating the fact that this had come up again. "Sorry. Sore subject. I also spent a lot of time abroad before the family got exiled."

She gasped and he frowned. Didn't she know what had

happened to his family?

"And that's when you became a Jaeger?" Lucy pressed.

"And that's when I became a Jaeger," he confirmed, letting out a long, slow sigh.

"Well, Mr. Jaeger," Lucy reached for his hand, bringing it up to cup her left breast. It fit well in his grasp. "Can you now confirm the rumor that you boasted about before—pleasing women with your touch?" She twisted her head to give him a peck on the cheek. "After all, it *is* my last night as a free woman and I want you to give me the pleasure that I hear only a Jaeger is capable of."

He shared her sweet smile and proceeded to do just that.

***

Gabriel snorted as he woke up to a pounding at the door.

"Jaeger Messenger? I'm sorry, but I'm afraid your time is up, sir," the guard said from the other side, his voice muffled. Gabriel glanced at the clock and swore under his breath as it was now past midnight. At least they had the decency to give him a little extra time before getting him.

"Yeah," he said, stretching out his arms as he sat up. "Give me a minute to get dressed, will ya?"

"Of course, sir. I'll be right here to collect Miss Spence once you're out."

Gabriel grumbled under his breath about the whole situation as he grabbed his black uniform trousers and then searched for his boots. Over the course of the night, he and Lucy brought each other to a couple more orgasms—screaming ones in her case. He hastily donned his uniform while Lucy sat up in a ball, wrapped in her bedsheets.

"Like you have anything to hide now?" he said wryly.

"Old habits, I guess," she said with a half-smile, letting the sheet drop enough for him to see her breasts one last time. "I guess I should get used to this look, huh?"

"Yeah," he said sadly as he buttoned his uniform top. Lucy slid off the bed, stood up, and helped him get the last clasp at his high collar. "Thank you," he said.

"I should be thanking you after everything that you've done for me," Lucy said, matching his sad smile. "I want you

58

to have something." She bent slightly while raising her left leg up, using him for support. Reaching down, she slid the garter down her thigh and off her leg before presenting it to him. "Typically, this is reserved for my husband who was supposed to take my maidenhead," she said, looking at it as if it contained some secret of the universe. "They're going to take it tomorrow anyway if I don't do something with it." She looked into his troubled eyes. "Since you're the one who took my virginity, I want you to have it."

Her hand shot up to his lips when he started to protest.

"Yes you can, and yes you will," she said with conviction. "This means a lot to me, and I'll go to the auction block with some comfort that at least one thing that I treasure in this world belongs to you. We have this night together and no one can take that from us."

"Dammit Lucy," Gabriel growled, feeling a pit of sadness develop in his gut.

"*Please,*" she pleaded with him, her big blue eyes begging him. "Please do this for me." She placed it in his hand and closed his fist around it, then kissed his knuckles softly. Once that was done, he finally nodded stiffly. "Thank you," she said with a small, resigned, smile.

"I swear to whatever god or gods that exists out there, I'm going to find a way to set you free," Gabriel said.

"I know you will." She leaned up and kissed him passionately on the lips. "Now go." She turned him and pushed him toward the door. "Just... don't look back at me when you leave. Please? I don't think that I could bear it."

Gabriel didn't think that he could bear it, either, even if he wanted to. If he did, he'd be tempted to draw his beamer and his blade then cut through the guards before they could react so he could rescue her. But he knew in his gut that wouldn't do either of them a damn bit of good. No, the best way was to pursue his investigation. With a shaking hand, he knocked on the door and the guard opened it, nodding politely at him albeit with a somber expression. Gabriel managed a dashing smile. "I really hope that these things are soundproof."

The guard was kind enough to laugh despite the graveness on each other's faces. "Don't worry, sir, we turn a polite ear away."

"Good man," he said with a tight smile. Gabriel marched by him, determined not to lose his resolve even though he could hear Lucy weeping as she was led back to her cell. Out of everyone in the cell block, she was probably the only innocent one here. As a Jaeger, he received a monthly report on the public auctions that listed out everyone's infractions so that buyers could determine who they wanted to take a chance and bid on since they were getting an inmate to house for a very long time, after all.

Because she was from the aristocracy, Lucy was listed as one of the premier auction options. Her reserve price was listed so high that Gabriel doubted that he'd seen that much gold in one place, let alone in his personal bank accounts... or the bank accounts of twenty Jaegers for that matter. So, buying Lucy was out of the question.

He couldn't buy her... there was no way he could afford her once the bidding started... but he knew someone who did have enough money and power to do it. And the man happened to owe Gabriel a few favors.

Once he was out of the building, he ran, but not toward home. With Lucy's garter still clutched in his fist, he didn't stop running until he was back to his office. The place was naturally deserted except for the few clockworks that marched around doing menial janitorial duties. He went straight to the office that he shared with Deliverer and picked up his telephone. After dialing the correct number, he waited as the operator put his call through. A minute later, the call was answered.

"Hello?"

"Hi, Deak? This is Gabriel."

"It's a little late, don't you think?" Deak asked, his voice sleepy.

"Yes, I know it's late and I apologize. I don't have time to talk much, but I'm calling in a solid. You really fucking owe me, and you have to move fast. Like be here in Atlanta yesterday, fast."

CHAPTER 8

"**U**p and at 'em!" the chief guard yelled as he moved cage to cage while rattling the bars with his club. "It's auction day and you inmates will be the first sold before we move to the voluntaries. You each have ten minutes to get cleaned up and doll yourself up the best you can before you're moved out."

Lucy didn't bother groaning or putting up a fuss like some of the other women in the adjoining cells were carrying on. She simply rolled out of her cot and trudged over to the pot in the corner to relieve herself. Then she took a quick, but cold, shower from the faucet that protruded from over the pot. After drying her body with the tattered blanket from the cot, she stood in front of the cracked mirror and opened the small back makeup box that had been left on the sink. Lucy opted for just a bit of eye shadow, blush, and ruby red lipstick. She had no desire to go overboard. Just as she finished, one of the guards returned to her cell.

"Let's go," he commanded her as he opened the cell.

Lucy complied with the order, walking out of the cell with her head down. The guard pulled her into the line of inmates on her side of the cell block and turned her to face forward. She was right in between two other women, both brunettes, one of which was trembling with apprehension and the other who had a guarded look on her face.

There was a sudden rustling of chains and then the snapping sound of metal clashing together. Alarmed, Lucy chanced a look forward. Four guards were coming down the line. One of them had manacles that he was slapping on the wrists of each prisoner. The one behind him placed his set of manacles around the ankles, and the final guard threaded a long chain through each set of manacles, from their collars, through the wrists, and down to the ankles. The free end was attached to the back of the next prisoner's collar. Lucy managed to crane her neck far enough to see that the inmate at the very front of the line had her free end of chain hanging off the wall like a lead.

Lucy's heart thudded in her chest as the guards got

closer to her. Finally, it was her turn, and in expert precision, they had her collared and manacled like everyone else. She was just another inmate in the line to be sold off into involuntary slave status. A nobody. She felt faint now that the cold iron touched her nude body. She started to hyper-ventilate.

Another guard came up to steady her, and placed hand on her shoulder. "Relax," he said in a calm, reassuring voice. "You'll be okay. Take some deep breaths and just focus on a point on the back of her head," he said, pointing to the girl in front of her.

Lucy swallowed hard and managed a shaky nod. "T-Thanks...."

He smiled before moving on down the line. She risked another glance and saw that he was giving the same instructions to others who were just as nervous as she was, if not more so. Across from her in the other line, the guards were in the process of shackling those women. *At least I'm not like that one girl over there,* Lucy thought as she observed a petite blonde wet herself the moment she was shackled and chained. The guards took it in stride and paused for a moment to scrub the girl down before continuing on.

Once the last of the prisoners was secured, the chief guard called out, "March!"

Taken off guard, Lucy was pulled forward. She stumbled, but managed to get into the right walking rhythm with everyone else. Her line was walked out first and the other line was placed into step behind them. They were led through the maze of corridors up a couple of levels before being ordered to halt in one exceptionally long and open hall. Then they were all ordered to face forward with their backs to one wall.

"Now, listen up, girls," the chief guard commanded. "Your collars serve a dual purpose: to remind you and others that you are, at your very core, an inmate. You are someone who has broken the law and will have to serve out your sentence. The other reason is to dissuade you from attempting to escape as no one in their right mind will help you remove your collar. If you ever attempt escape, the Jaegers will find you..."

Lucy tuned him out, disinterested in what the collars did

as she had no desire to ever escape. Her fate now was far preferable to what awaited her otherwise. So, she just stood there in line, feeling morose, until the chief guard finished his spiel and moved on.

Minutes later, a distinguished-looking Consortium official with a couple of aides marched down the line of soon-to-be slaves, checking numbers on collars against a list. Lucy was a bit disappointed that it wasn't Mr. Muller.

"Lot five-nineteen," she heard him call out while he glanced at the brunette ahead of her. "Contract Number I.S. zero zero eight three one zero one zero five zone nine. Chloe Craith, no real domestic skills, assigned as a pleasure slave. Starting bid of one hundred gold." He handed a quill pen and a parchment to her and pointed to the bottom. "Sign here, please."

"Um, what if I don't want to sign?" she asked in a tiny voice, uncertain at the terms laid out before her.

The official sighed as if he heard that line a million times. "Then we yank you out of line and you go to the place that the judge in your case sentenced you to."

Wide-eyed, the girl hastily grabbed the pen and signed, tip scratching against the parchment contract.

"Thank you," he said, handing the signed parchment over to one aide and getting a new one from his other aide.

They stepped forward in front of Lucy. One aide lifted her chin to look at the number on her collar while the official started talking. "Lot five-twenty. Contract Number I.S. zero zero eight three one zero one zero five two zero. Lucy Spence, no real domestic skills. Assigned as a pleasure slave. Starting bid of one hundred gold." The parchment and quill were thrust toward her, and the official pointed at the bottom where there was a line with her name underneath. "Sign here, please."

Lucy's bright blue eyes scanned the document. It didn't really contain anything that she wasn't expecting. With no skills beyond some basic domestic (and even that was a stretch), she was fit only to be a pleasure slave and serve at the whims of a purchasing master who could then sell or trade her at will, and she was to remain such for the length of her sentence of ten years. Her heart sank. Ten years! She'd be

63

a slave until she was almost forty. But, considering that a breeder camp was her only other option, the choice was easy. Lucy grabbed the quill and signed without hesitation.

The Consortium official thanked her and went on to the next woman in line and Lucy's thoughts drifted, blocking out everything and wondering again why she was being punished for deeds that her brother had done.

She had always tried to be a good daughter and did as she was instructed, but that had obviously gotten her nowhere. She was in this predicament now because she had followed what her brother dictated. Then, in order to keep her family's name clean, she cooperated fully with the Consortium Jaegers since they were, after all, the supreme law of the land and her teachings told her that she was to respect all authority. But, somewhere along the line she was made out to be the villain in all of this. Why?

A second official came down the line. He held a boxy device with two antennae on the top in his hands; he was studying it intently. This got Lucy's attention. She watched as the man stopped every so often in front of a slave, frowned, made a couple of adjustments to the instrument, and then did something to the back of the collar before moving on. He paused in front of her, adjusted the small screen he was looking at again, and then reached up behind Lucy's neck to run his brass-encased fingers along the metal that was touching her neck. Lucy let out a tiny yelp as the collar shocked her just a bit after he pulled away.

"What was that for?" she asked, glaring at him while trying to rub the spot.

"Just a small deterrent in case you ever get the insane notion of running," he replied causally.

Lucy snorted. "Like I have anywhere to go now...."

Images of her being used sexually by men from nearby mining and lumber towns for the sole purpose of breeding ran through her head, causing her to shudder. It was like Gabriel said—this, at least, was a little bit better than that notion.

The official chuckled. "Well then, you won't have anything to worry about, will you?" he asked before moving on down the line.

***

Prod. Shuffle forward. Stop and wait. Prod. Shuffle forward. Stop and wait. It had been like this for the past hour.

The nineteen other girls in front of Lucy were auctioned off at a variety of sums. Listening in while they were in line waiting to be sold off, Lucy learned that their crimes ranged from petty theft to trespassing to flagrantly being out past curfew. One young woman proudly stated that she was busted for streaking naked out of her home into public and that she wanted to be sold off rather than be under the thumb of her oppressive family. Every so often, after the line moved and stopped, the others would try to engage her to find out what she'd done, but Lucy remained quiet as she was ashamed to even be in this situation to begin with. Her silence seemed to enhance the mystery around her and the girls started speculating what she'd done. Eventually, Lucy just tuned them out as they were prodded farther and farther along as each girl spent her time on the block.

There were five more young women behind her, followed by the men who were convicted of a multitude of crimes ranging from burglary to minor fisticuffs. Where the women would be used for domestic work or pleasure slaves, the men would more than likely be heading for hard labor.

When her turn arrived, her collar chain was disconnectted from the girl behind her and she was taken by her arm out into the main theater. Her eyes were assaulted by the bright lights that shined upon the stage, illuminating every feature she had to offer, and making it so she was unable to see the audience. The guard led her out to center stage where she stepped up onto a small platform. She stood there in wide-eyed fright and figured that she was quite the sight; standing there fully nude with her golden locks spilling down her back, her wrists manacled before her, causing her arms to press her breasts together to jut out, and her dolled up face with a mask of fear on it. Somehow, she managed to keep from shaking or fainting.

The guard left and the auctioneer stepped up. "Lot five-twenty, folks," he said in a clear, booming voice. "Former Theocracy noblewoman. Sentenced ten years. Pleasure slave

65

with no domestic skills. Starting bid is one hundred gold."

Much to her surprise, the bidding for her exploded from the audience immediately. Bids were shouted so fast, and the auctioneer talked even faster. Lucy had no idea how much she was going for. One by one, the calls fell off as the price grew higher than the audience members could handle. After ten minutes of calling out bids, it came down to two people in the back row going back and forth.

"A thousand five!" a man shouted. Lucy thought she detected some desperation in his voice.

"A thousand twenty," another man yelled out, sounding calm and bored.

Lucy couldn't help but blink in amazement. Her price was now in the thousands? Just for her?

"A thousand twenty-five," the desperate man countered.

"A thousand fifty," the bored man said without hesitation.

"A thousand fifty-five!"

"Eleven hundred."

The tennis match of bidding between the two continued with Desperate Man raising five every time Bored Man made a bid in increments of twenty to fifty.

Finally, something snapped in Bored Man as he clipped out in a harsh voice, "Two thousand, five hundred. Beat it or go home to your little prison, Anderson!"

Lucy gasped. Was that the same Anderson who had been at her trial? It had to be, as the Bored Man called him out on going back to a prison. Her breath hitched and she started to hyperventilate knowing that Desperate Man was actually Overseer Anderson and he was still bent on taking her back to that breeder farm!

She wanted to scream, rant, and rave about the unfairness of it all. How was it possible that she could fall into the same lot that Gabriel should have ensured that she avoid? Now she was facing it all over again. It wasn't fair! She felt faint, but managed to keep standing. Now, she just hoped that whoever Bored Man was, he would win.

Anderson seemed to fluster and blubber from somewhere off to Lucy's right. "I bid...," he started to say.

"I don't give a damn what you bid because I'll match it

66

every damn time and raise it even higher just because you're pissing me off!" Bored Man now thundered. "You're drawing this out when we both know that you're going to lose. Go home, little man!"

"Two thousand, five hundred and five!" Anderson persisted.

"Three thousand! Want to keep this up? No? Then get out!"

The auctioneer watched the exchange with amusement. "I got three thousand to Lord Michaelson. Is there a raise on that? Anyone? No? Then, going once, going twice, sold for three thousand gold!" The auctioneer banged the gavel to end the auction.

The enormity of the situation now weighed on her more so than ever before. She was now the legal property of whoever Lord Michaelson was. The name was familiar to her, but she was too much in a daze as the guard returned to lead her off the stage. At least she wasn't going to be owned by Overseer Anderson. That, at least, was a small relief.

Another guard stepped out opposite from where she'd been led in, took her by the arm, and led her off the stage. Her mind whirled and spun as she was taken to a small, side room. The guard sat her down at a small desk, latching her collar to a chain to keep her in place. Then, she was left alone.

Lucy shivered with apprehension as she could do nothing but stare at the point on the desk in front of her where her leash was locked. A multitude of questions flew through her head. What was her owner like? What was he going to expect of her? What was he going to do to her? She'd heard stories of what happened to pleasure slaves—voluntary or otherwise—but she just didn't know for certain and it was tearing her apart inside. And how long was her new owner going to take to get here?

A sudden rattling at the door to the holding room made her jump and she stared at it with wide-eyed fright as it creaked open. The Consortium official who had taken her information was showing in another man.

"Here you go, Lord Michaelson. Lot five-twenty, Lucy Spence. Please confirm that the number on your copy of the contract matches that on her collar and then sign here above her signature."

Well, at least he's handsome looking in a rugged sort of way, Lucy conceded as the tall, trim, dark-haired man took the contract. He was dressed as impeccably as the Consortium official. Without any preamble, he gently pushed Lucy's head forward a bit so that he could get a good look at the back of her collar.

"India sierra zero zero eight three one zero one zero five two zero," he recited as he compared the engraved number to what was written on his contract. His voice was as smooth as silk and she found herself warming up to him with just that. "Yes, it matches." He placed the signed contract on the small table in front of Lucy and scrawled out his name, which Lucy saw as Deacon Michaelson.

Deacon looked her over with an appraising glare, rubbing his chin thoughtfully in the process. "I must say that you've got to be the most expensive slave maid I've ever purchased," he commented as the Consortium official took his keys and unlocked the handle of her leash to hand to him.

Confused, Lucy blinked as her manacles were then removed from her wrists. "You... you're not going to use me as a pleasure slave?" she asked, shocked.

Deacon cocked his head slightly and arched his eyebrow. "Do you want me to?" he asked, a twinge of amusement in his voice. "Don't get me wrong, I would definitely have fun with it as you are all kinds of pleasing to the eye."

Lucy blushed and Deacon chuckled.

"Let's just say that I don't intend to use you as purchased and leave it at that."

Now Lucy was really confused; it was totally out of character for any man in the Theocracy to pass on sexual rights to a slave in their ownership. "Then why did you buy me?"

His gaze and his voice turned hard. "Because I hate being indebted to someone and my agreement to buy you and look after you fulfills my long-standing debt to a certain Jaeger who we both know. Now, come along," he said, picking up her leash. "We'll get you to my estate where you'll start learning your new job."

CHAPTER 9

The next morning, Gabriel was in his Consortium office reviewing his reports and intelligence dispatches for the day before moving on to his pet project. The only problem was that his heart just wasn't in the normal workload today. Reaching into his pocket, he took out Lucy's garter. He held it up at eye level to study it while resting on one elbow. *She's Deacon's now...,* he thought sullenly. *At least he'll treat her decently like she deserves....*

The whole case stank. What was the deal with that judge? Something that was just a minor infraction and should've been a slap on the wrist at the worst, but he sentences an innocent girl to a breeder farm? Ten years, at that. Absurd! His thoughts were interrupted when Jake Walker came in and tossed a newssheet down in front of him.

"Morning, Gabe. There's another headline in there about girls going missing from New Mobile," he said cordially. Jake looked at him and caught him staring at the garter and grinned. "You wind up going to a wedding yesterday as well? Or, is that from an admirer of yours?"

"Huh?" Gabriel asked. "This? Oh. It's uh... from a friend."

He barely gave the newssheet a glance as he had more pressing matters on his mind. He gave Deliverer a sideways look. He was being chipper this morning, but then again, he'd just closed a major case and been partying at a wedding.

"Some friend if they're giving you their garter," Jake said with a smirk and a wink.

"Actually, she's an iSlave now," Gabriel said defensively, with a little more bite than he'd intended. "She just got sold yesterday at open market."

"Oh," Jake said, suddenly abashed. "Sorry. Do you, uh, want to talk about it?"

Gabriel shrugged it off. "Don't worry about it. I'm just pissed that I lost her case. By all rights, it should've been an easy win. Anyway, there's a note there from Muller on your desk. He referred the case to you since you're our resident expert on the matter." Gabriel pointed while finally reaching for the newssheet to read the headlines.

Jake thanked him and walked over to the desk that he used when he was in Atlanta. There was a bundle of pics tied together with twine waiting for his review. Jake turned over the note that fellow Jaeger, Coleton Muller, had left on top of it.

"Last night, Director Ambrose Wain of the First National Bank of Dixie was assassinated," he muttered as he read. "Son of a bitch. The other suspect is no longer at large. The attack has been determined to have been carried out by Cheyenne and her corsairs per the images captured by on scene security flashers. Damn," he said, crushing the note in his fist.

Jake pulled at the twine holding the bundle together and started sifting through the pics like a man possessed. Gabriel ignored him as Jake became engrossed in chasing down his career obsession.

Every Jaeger had one. For Jake, it was Cheyenne. Shadow had brought down the Von Vyners and it'd made his career. Emancipator gallivanted along the Dixie-Corporate States-Wastelands borders hunting down a man named Auctor Frost. And, right now, Gabriel's obsession was Judge Takacy. He tossed the newssheet aside, slid Lucy's garter around his wrist, and reached for the telephone on his desk where he dialed up the office secretary. Jaegers typically worked alone, but they did have offices manned with support staff to help them wherever they went.

"Yeah, Grace? Can you get me as many of the court cases that you can on Judge Takacy here in the Theocracy?" he asked. Gabriel came up from Elysium to the Theocracy so often that he was on a first name basis with everyone here. "And, while you're at it, can you get Goliath on the phone for me, please? I need to call this one in to start a new investigation. And tell them to hurry so I can get started. Thanks."

As his fellow Jaeger was swearing and cursing up a storm over at his desk before he tore out of the office like the devil was on his heels, Gabriel hung up the phone and started making notes of his own while he waited for his call to go through.

70

Ten minutes later, Grace called back. "Sir, Shadow is on the line for you."

Wow... the big man himself, Gabriel thought as the call got switched over. On the other end, the head of Jaeger operations for all North and Central America was waiting. "This had better be really important to get me up early," Shadow said with a yawn.

"I'm, uh, sorry sir. I wasn't expecting you," Gabriel admitted while glancing at the chronometer on the wall. "Umm, it's actually the start of normal business hours... sir."

"I am entitled to a vacation on occasion, ya know." Shadow laughed ruefully. "Huntress is out on extended patrol, Goliath is out on an investigation, and more of our Jaegers in your chain of command are out on various assignments. I was the only person that H.Q. could reach in such a hurry since your secretary said it was urgent. So, don't stress over it too much. What'cha got?"

"A Theocracy judge by the name of Takacy, sir," Gabriel said. "He tried a case recently for a Miss Lucy Spence in which he rendered a guilty verdict and tried to override Consortium law by getting her sentenced to a breeder farm up north, despite her opting for iSlave status after the ruling. You, uh, might remember her from her older brother's recent case, of which Deliverer and I were assigned."

"Yes, and as I recalled no charges were levied against Miss Spence," Shadow said, sounding more alert.

"True—that was a deal brokered by one of our accountants who was here investigating the Carmichael finances. A one Lucas Wolverton."

"I've heard of him," Shadow replied with a pained voice. "But, still, why was Miss Spence brought to trial? She turned evidence for us in exchange for immunity."

"She was brought to trial at the Theocracy level, sir. Not the Consortium level," Gabriel replied. He heard Shadow let loose a tirade of swearing that'd make and airship crewman blush on the other end. Gabriel let him finish before moving on. "It was trumped up charges from her family's former lawyer. I don't have proof... yet... but I have a gut feeling that the D.A. and the judge were in on this. They sped the trial through so fast that I barely had time to get there to act as advocate."

"You've got to be kidding me," Shadow groaned on the other end, sounding weary. "And you think this judge has something shady going on?"

"Well, you *do* know the old joke, right? What do you call a hundred Theocracy judges at the bottom of the ocean?"

"A good start," Shadow chuckled. "Alright, Messenger, your intuition has served you well in the past. You've got a green light to pursue this one." There was a pause on the other end. "Out of curiosity, what did happen to Miss Spence?"

"I managed to get this judge to agree to iSlave status for her by threatening a high-level investigation. But, ever since I've said that, coupled with the fact that they've denied all my filed appeals in record time for the Theocracy, investigating him feels like the right thing to do. I know that I would've had to get approval after the fact to start the investigation right then and there, but I couldn't let her be unjustly sentenced like that." Gabriel involuntarily winced, glad that his boss couldn't see him through the phone lines.

"Think nothing of it. You were right in doing that. If the Theocracy creates an issue out of it, I got a few friends on their Security Council that'll put an end to it. So, where is Miss Spence now?"

Well, that was good considering that their Supreme Court was probably filing their protest as they spoke. "She was auctioned off yesterday as a pleasure slave, sir. I called in a favor to an old friend of mine to buy her since I know that he'd treat her well."

"Some favor. You didn't purchase her yourself?" Shadow sounded amused.

"Not unless you want to authorize me one helluva raise, sir. A former noblewoman here in the Theocracy? There was no way I would've been able to come close to the opening bid, let alone the three grand that she sold for. That might not come close to what her bride price would've been for a free noblewoman, but it's still a hefty amount."

"Fair enough. Tread carefully on this one. Minor nobles and the average populace is one thing up there. Going after a judge, though? Make sure your case is solid. If he is crooked like you think he is, then we should be able to get his ruling

72

overturned and get your girlfriend free."

How the hell does he know that? Gabriel wondered. "I never said..."

Shadow laughed. "You didn't have to. I can hear it in your voice—you have a thing for this girl. Can't say that I blame you. Lucy Spence is smokin' hot."

"How?" He glanced around the office wondering if there was a flasher or even one of those new moving picture takers around, spying on him. Then Gabriel quickly decided that he didn't actually want to know how Shadow knew. You didn't get to be regional head of the Jaegers by being clueless, and that man seemed to know everything. "Never mind. Thank you, sir. Sorry about disturbing you on vacation, sir." With that, he hung up the phone.

Grace came in with a box full of files, and a couple of clockworks in tow carrying two more a piece. She put them on the corner of Gabriel's desk with a huff before directing the clockworks to drop the other boxes there. "Here you are, sir," she said, wiping her sweating brow that was matted with her raven hair.

"Thanks." Gabriel looked at her and the line of clockworks. "That was quick."

"This is just the first load of boxes, sir," she said in her sweet Dixie accent. "These were just the ones that I could easily find here in the Consortium offices. We have more comin' from the basement and more still comin' from the Dixie court archives this afternoon."

Gabriel thanked her again as he reached for the first file. Then he paused as a thought occurred to him. He looked her up and down, assessing her very conservative dull green dress that kept her upper arms covered and went down to cover everything, including her feet. "Grace, you're from here in the Theocracy, right?"

"Umm, yessir." She gulped, a flash of fear in her eyes.

"Relax, you're not in trouble or anything, but I am wondering—is every girl around here nowadays taught that they should not speak up against a man? And, if she does, it is that something that typically warrants a trial?"

"Oh, no, sir!" Grace exclaimed, eyes wide at her outburst. She immediately corrected herself into a more subdued posture. "No, sir. Usually if a woman has to bear witness, we just tell our men and then they decide if they are going to sponsor us... that's uh... granting us permission to speak and taking any blame should something go wrong.... Or, they testify on their woman's behalf." She shrugged. "Usually, if a lady talks out of turn like Miss Spence did, then it's just a slap on the wrist, forbidding them to go out into public, or something of the like by their men."

"But bringing them to trial?"

Grace gave another shrug. "Unusual, maybe, but not totally unheard of... especially at the end of the month close to auction time." She frowned and cocked her head. "Shouldn't you know all this, being a lawyer and all?"

"I usually handle the bigger, high profile cases for capital offenses. Something like this is normally considered so small that it flies under my radar. But, now it has me thinking," Gabriel admitted. "You heard about Miss Spence's trial?"

She looked abashed and even darted her eyes around to make sure no one else was listening. "Sir, everyone heard about that one," she whispered. "A noblewoman in trouble for speaking up? My own father used that as an example for me to keep quiet." She then blushed. "I-I'm sorry, sir, I-I shouldn't have said anything."

He waved her off. "Don't worry about it. Your secret is safe with me. After all, I did ask." Another thought occurred to him. "Why does your father allow you to work?"

She looked embarrassed by that question. "Because it's not like we're a big noble family, sir, with lotsa money. We have mouths to feed at home and we all need to work."

Gabriel released a huff of air as he reached for a stylus and a sheaf of paper to start taking notes. "You wives be beholden to your own husbands so that even if any of them are disobedient to the word they may be won without a word by the behavior of their wives...," he grumbled, quoting directly from the One Book that the Theocracy of Dixie used as the basis for all their laws. Gabriel wondered what Saint Peter would've thought about his words being used in such a way or Paul knowing that this reference, in accordance to his own letter to the city of Corinth, would've been used years after his own death. *Probably would've cheered the fact and*

74

declared these people to be good, wholesome, men..., Gabriel thought ruefully as he started to pour over the court records.

The hours dragged on and the more he looked at the records, the grimmer a picture was being painted. Takacy normally stayed up in the Kentucky Providence where he reigned supreme as far as Theocracy judges were concerned. He was the ultimate authority in terms of both rank and seniority.

"So, why did they pull you all the way down here into the Georgia Providence for this one trial?" Gabriel wondered out loud as he reviewed, line by line, the synopsis of every trial Takacy ever tried. The majority were the Theocracy versus some poor woman with no representation, and the outcome was the same each time—guilty with sentencing to Taylorsville where that overseer was located.

Glancing up at the golden-brown map of the continent on the far wall, Gabriel did some mental calculations. Taylorsville was a good way up in the Appalachian Mountains right on the border of the Kentucky and Carolina Providences. It was nestled on a peak approximately halfway between the respective providence capitols of Lexington and Charlotte. Aside from the women's prison, there was an abundance of lumber and mining camps in the area.

"Why ship women and entertainment in when you can have it right there in the middle of it all?" Gabriel mused.

He imagined morale was high in those work camps. That thought nagged at him and he asked Grace to also have the clerks pull up the prison records from Taylorsville. She regarded him with a funny look but went to do his bidding regardless.

"Call it a hunch," Gabriel said as he dove back into Takacy's trial history.

This... was going to take a while. He got up and got some coffee with enough caffeine to keep an airship crew going indefinitely.

***

In the following weeks, the more that Gabriel delved into his investigation, the uglier things became. Prominent families

75

were conducting virtual witch hunts to gain assets that the others controlled, middle-class women and noblewomen were forced into breeder camps to drop bride prices in a region down, and then there was the simple fact that under Theocracy law, a man could just knock a girl up and force them into wedlock. After all, why pay a high price for a virginal wife when you can just go get one used down at the local prison for a quarter amount of the gold?

Gabriel turned in his chair to add another piece of evidence to his wall that was slowly becoming covered with information. There was a map of the Theocracy with arrows going back and forth from Atlanta up to Taylorsville. Then, another arrow from Taylorsville to the Wastelands with a big question mark.

According to the most recent prison records, some iSlaves that were sent up north to Taylorsville were unaccounted for, and there had been increased raider and pirate activity in the area up there. It was a pretty steady stream of attacks that always seemed to just miss a Dixie Air Corps patrol or a Jaeger being in the area. What was worse was that the missing iSlaves weren't reported missing until days after the fact.

On a hunch, Gabriel got on the phone and called one of his closest friends within the Consortium, Lincoln Powell, Jaeger Emancipator.

"Y'ello?" Lincoln's deep voice came in from the other end.

"Hey, it's Messenger down in Atlanta. Ya got a minute?" Gabriel asked, thankful that Lincoln was back in the country and not out in the Wastelands where he normally liked to operate.

"Always, man. What can I do ya for?"

"iSlaves that go missing from Taylorsville Penitentiary... have you ever recovered any of them?"

There was hesitation on the other end followed by an irritated huff of air. "No. By the time the attacks happen from out of the Wastelands by Auctor Frost and his little trio fleet of ramshackle airships, it's too late to get up there. No one reports their initial sightings because they fly up the Ohio River Valley, practically skimming the water, and hang a

76

sharp right just before they get to the ruins of Louisville," Lincoln explained. "The Corporate States think they're going for Dixie and Dixie thinks they're going for the Corporate States."

"Interesting...," Gabriel commented, taking notes on his pad as Lincoln talked. "But, what about their transponders that are in their collars?"

"They're not activated," Lincoln replied. "By the time Taylorsville reports the missing iSlaves, its days after the fact and they report that they've already turned the control batons in to the Consortium Offices here in Lexington. It's like bureaucracy at its worst up there... I've been trying to combat it for years now." He paused on the other end. "You got a line on something else happening here?"

"Right now, I have a growing theory about what's going on since I have a judge down here in Atlanta constantly funneling girls off the street up there toward you," Gabriel said. "And, a lot of them have then conveniently gone missing from Taylorsville, provided they're not just bought up by the local populace."

"Yeah, the locals here love 'em," Lincoln admitted. "Why try to woo and marry a girl when you can just buy one's contract, knock 'em up, and—*boom*—instant wife. It's been keeping the bride price down all over the Theocracy, especially those who couldn't afford one otherwise."

"Yeah... I was just thinking the same thing," Gabriel said. "Alright, thanks for your time, Emancipator. Can you give me a ring the next time the raiders hit up there? I'm trying to get a timeline down."

"Not a problem so long as you come up here and help with them," Lincoln agreed at once. "I figure that Frosty is due to attack any day now as it's been a couple of months since his last attack."

"Will do, thanks." Gabriel hung up the phone and then furrowed his brow as he wrote down the timetable. He then compared it to when Takacy was down in Atlanta to hear cases and when Anderson was down to collect girls from him. All of the attacks seemed to run a few days to a week from when Anderson had a good gaggle of girls to take back with him, also in the middle of Takacy's month of sitting on the bench in Atlanta. It gave Takacy plausible deniability, but painted Anderson in a really suspicious light.

He checked his notes on Anderson's whereabouts. According to the recent report he'd gotten from the Ghost Jaeger that was tailing the man, Anderson skipped town shortly after the open auction. That was another thing that stuck out in Gabriel's mind as he consulted a book on the auctions for the past year—Anderson was present at every single one at the end of the month and made a few purchases. Those women were then taken up to Taylorsville and some of those were among the missing.

"How the hell did you fly under the radar for so long?" Gabriel muttered as he wrote down even more damning notes. He was missing the piece of the puzzle that tied this back to Takacy. He shifted tactics and started following the paper trail again on Takacy's court cases, going through each one that came up in no particular order. *I'm going to have to have a word with the clerks,* he thought as he picked up a five-year old case, and then another that was seven, and then another that was merely a year old. *These go back at least ten years and are just scattered about...*

Gabriel picked up the next file in his seemingly unending stack. His blood ran cold and his hand shook hard when he saw the names: *Theocracy of Dixie vs Connor, Abigail, Gabriel and Adeline McKibben.*

"Holy shit...," he gasped, blinking as he read the case notes. He, his parents, and his sister were all named as litigants when the Spences ruined them. He didn't know much about the case as he'd been hiding out with the Michaelsons at the time before skipping out of the country to Elysium to join the Consortium.

His eyes darted over the words on the papers as he read the absurd charges ranging from breaking faith with God all the way to more hefty allegations of delinquency on multiple accounts, bankruptcy, and treason due to allowing their little slice of the Theocracy to be underdefended.

"That's when I transferred the assets to Deak to keep them out of the Spence's hands...," Gabriel Said, seething. He had no idea all this had gone down. The Consortium expunged his record as they often do in refugee cases, and

78

when he returned to his home country as a Jaeger, the Theocracy couldn't touch him.

Grabbing a book that held the full Taylorsville roster, Gabriel furiously flipped through it to compare the numbers that the court had assigned his family with those of the inmates. He found all three of them with no problem. His sister had been the only one to be considered for iSlave status after getting there, but she was listed as deceased due to suicide. That, he knew. What got him was that his father had died doing hard labor on a chain gang while his mother eventually just wasted away after he passed by refusing to eat. He'd known that they'd died while imprisoned, but he never knew the circumstances.

Pain ached in his heart as he closed his eyes and winced at the memories. It just hardened his resolve to break up this little ring that Takacy, Anderson, and now this Auctor Frost fellow seemed to have going on.

"Are you okay, sir?" Grace's meek voice came from the doorway.

Gabriel opened his eyes and blinked the tears away that had started welling up from the painful past. "Yeah, Grace," he croaked in a hollow voice as he made a show of checking the time. "It's just late... that's all. Why don't you check out and get back to your family?"

"I still have an hour, sir."

He waved her off. "Go... I'll authorize it as administrative leave. Give your family my best."

"O... okay. Thank you!" Grace responded, suddenly happy.

Gabriel gave her a brave smile as he watched her go. *At least someone here can still enjoy a family...* he mused as his eyes drifted back down to the court documents. Part of him wanted to be upset with himself for not doing anything about his own family's untimely demise, but the other part of him remembered his father's words: *Our fates are sealed, but you still have a chance. Go to the Consortium and make sure this doesn't happen to good people ever again.*

"I will, dad...," Gabriel muttered to his father's ghost as he dove back into his investigation.

79

CHAPTER 10

Two days later, Gabriel received word that a raider airship was steaming its way up the Ohio River. Now that word was out about what Auctor Frost's trio was up to, they were relatively easy to spot. With the help of Coleton Muller and Jaeger Intruder, in his new Bell-Carmichael Devastator II, Gabriel got a quick ride up north by hanging underneath the right-wing bomb rack. As they circled high above the Ohio River just west of the Theocracy border town of Paducah, Emancipator joined them by flying up with his armor's flight pack. He locked into place on the bomb rack underneath the left wing and cut his engines.

"Fancy meeting you ladies here," he quipped with a quick salute of his brass gauntlet.

"Wouldn't miss it," Gabriel responded through the radio. "So, where's our boy?"

"Coming up from the Memphis Ruins at the north end of the Bay," Lincoln said, checking a display on his left wrist. "I figure that we have a few minutes before they come around the bend," he said and pointed off toward the west.

"Well, we can wait," Coleton added from the cockpit. "I charge by the minute, anyway."

They all shared a laugh which helped loosen them up in the otherwise tense moments leading up to an engagement. Five minutes later, Coleton called out the contact.

"Tallyho! One fugly looking airship at nine o'clock low! Is that y'all's buddy?"

Lincoln looked in that direction, a reticle coming down over his helmet where his right eye would be. It telescoped out as he studied the ship. "Yup. The *Airship Henosis*. The blue-white starburst emblem on the back tailfin is the dead giveaway. Many people confuse it with the Corporates State's ice and refrigeration company, Polar Ice, but the difference is that Frost puts it against a sandy background with flecks of red mixed in to represent the sand and blood of the Wastelands," he explained.

"If you know so much about this guy, how come you haven't bagged him yet?" Gabriel asked jokingly, knowing full well that catching Consortium's most wanted was easier said than done.

"Remind me—how long has Deliverer gone after Cheyenne and how long did Shadow go after Vyner?" Lincoln countered, holding his armor-encased middle finger toward Gabriel.

"Eh... good point," Gabriel conceded.

"If you two are done gabbing down there," Coleton interjected, "how you wanna play this?"

"We could always ask them to land," Gabriel snickered.

"Oh, hey, yeah, then we can have tea and fuckin' crumpets while we're at it!" Lincoln replied sarcastically. "You think they're gonna just heave to and let us board 'em?"

"We could ask."

"Oh sure, we could ask."

Gabriel could hear the eyeroll and sigh in Lincoln's voice.

Lincoln chimed in the broadband radio. "*Airship Henosis,* this is Jaeger Emancipator of the Consortium. Land immediately and stand by to be boarded at once."

Below them, the airship seemed to pause as its old-fashioned propeller engines cut off and it drifted forward on inertia. Then it slowly and laboriously turned in place. Three white lights in the aft of the ship then lit off as the airship engaged its Tesla engines and tried to make a dart to the northwest.

"Well... so much for that idea."

"Fine... we do this the hard way," Gabriel said.

"Good, I like the hard way," Coleton replied, pulling the Devastator around and into a screaming dive for the top of the airship. "I'll buzz the bow of the ship and drop you two off on the way by. You should be able to find a window to bust through while I have their attention."

"I like it," Gabriel said, checking his arm cannon and making sure that it was charged and ready to shoot.

Like their beamer sidearms, the arm cannons shaved off pieces of a metal block, formed it into a small metal ball, charged it, and shot it out at high velocity. It was a *fuck you, fuck your cover, fuck the five guys behind you, and fuck whatever the hell you all were standing in front of* kind of weapon. It turned men into goo and could take care of most aerial vehicles. In small groups, they'd been known to bring down low-flying airships.

As they closed in, the *Henosis* started things off by firing at them from a ball turret on the back end of the ship where the massive rudder met the horizontal stabilizers. Coleton responded in kind, blowing the turret away.

"Solves that problem of worrying if they were really aggressors or not," he quipped as he pulled up and flew along the spine of the airship.

"You fucking doubted me?" Lincoln snorted.

"Just a little...," Coleton snickered. "Here's your stop!" He pulled a lever on the side of his seat to release the bomb clamps that held the other two Jaegers under his wings. "Thank you for flying Intruder Air!"

"Screw you!" Gabriel called back as he unfurled his suit's wings while he dropped in the air. He banked left, flying down alongside of the *Henosis* and following the bulbous tisigen tanks around. He spied a portside window, aimed his arm, and clenched his fist, firing a single shot into the side of the ship. The window blew inward and there was a rush of air out as the pressurized air escaped in a *whoosh*. It wasn't as forceful as he'd expected and he figured that Lincoln was already doing the same on the starboard side of the airship.

Gabriel pointed his feet, which engaged the engine on his back in a short, quick burst of speed. He shot into the opening he created, flipping at the last minute to impact on the wall, leaving a massive dent. Landing on the deck on his feet, he tracked his arm cannon around and sent a whole row of raiders to their maker when they pulled weapons on him. Then he turned on his heel and headed forward to the bridge. He grabbed the hatch and ripped it clean off its hinges, pointing his cannon inside.

"Consortium! Hands in the air!" he shouted through his microphone.

A guard on the bridge got that gleam in his eye and Gabriel put a fiery hole the size of a grapefruit through him and the bulkhead beyond without a second thought.

On the other side of the bridge, Lincoln shouted the same thing as he came in. Seeing that they were flanked and outgunned, the ragtag-looking raiders slowly raised their hands in surrender. Gabriel keyed his radio while Lincoln started rounding up the crew to force them to the back of the bridge.

"Intruder, this is Messenger; we have the *Henosis*."

"Awww, and y'all didn't even save me some...," Coleton mock whined back at him.

"Roger that, returning to base then. See you when you get that slow ass thing back to the barn."

***

Hours later, Gabriel entered the interrogation room that held the captain of the *Henosis*, and tossed his folder of evidence onto the table. He sat down at the table.

They'd flown the airship to Lexington and took the command crew to the Consortium Offices in the city while the rest of the crew was dispersed around the local constable offices to await holding and trial.

"You've already been advised of your rights and the reason for the arrest, yes? So here is what we have," Gabriel told the man who was shackled with his hands behind the chair as he made a show of examining the file. "Your airship has been flagged on multiple counts of air piracy. Jaeger Emancipator's mountain of evidence alone is enough to have you and your whole crew shot without a trial. Ah, ah, ah," he said and held up a forestalling hand when the man opened his mouth. "Don't try to insult my intelligence by saying that you're just some innocent merchant. We've already run your ship through the Theocracy and Corporate States registries and they both came back that you're a raider."

Gabriel set the folder down, folded his hands on the table, and looked at the raider captain. "Here are your options. Option A: you talk, you give me your boss' location, you answer all of my questions that I have about your activities with Taylorsville, and we can get you a plea deal. A Consortium prison up in Greenland, or maybe one in the Australian outback where you'll spend the rest of your life. Option B: I make you talk and maybe kill you later if I don't like your answers. As for the final option...." Gabriel pulled his beamer and set it on the table. "We could just skip the Q and A session and the paperwork altogether." Gabriel gave him a big smile.

The captain eyed the beamer and then looked at Gabriel. "I'll talk!" He nodded enthusiastically. "I'll talk."

"Good," Gabriel nodded. He noticed beads of sweat had started to develop all over the man's forehead. "Good! Open dialogue is good for civilization, don't you think? Let's start with the ten chests full of gold that we found in your hold." Gabriel took the pic out of the folder. "Usually, it's the other way around. Raiders take gold from the civilized countries back to the Wastelands—they don't take gold from the Wastelands into the Theocracy. In my book, that's a payoff. Who's it for?"

"Overseer Anderson in Taylorsville," the captain replied at once, now breathing hard. "We make like we're raiding the place, take the women back to the Wastes, leave the gold. That's how the arrangement always is. He supplies us with women, we supply him with gold."

Which Anderson, no doubt, then uses to get more girls at auction and uses it as a payoff to Takacy, Gabriel thought as he documented everything the man said. "Just women in general?" Gabriel asked.

"Sometimes," the captain shrugged. "A lot of times we have a list of preferences. Noblewomen are always good to breed with, and it gives our warlords a shot at legitimacy."

"Interesting...." Gabriel commented as he jotted that tidbit down, not bothering to mention to the man that any women who are taken into the Wastelands lose their standing almost immediately, so children produced by such unions wouldn't have claims to any Theocracy assets. "How's Anderson getting the women for you all?"

Another shrug. "Got me. We don't care where he gets 'em from just so long as he gets 'em for us."

Gabriel frowned and made a little sound of disappointment. It was a longshot question to implicate Takacy and it fell short. "No knowledge of where your gold is going?"

"Again, we don't care so long as he gets the goods."

"How do you all know when to come to the Theocracy for your little... raid?" Gabriel eyed him.

"The boss says to come, we come."

"Anderson or Frost?"

"Anderson calls Frost. Frost tells us to go," the captain said.

"And you know that Anderson is calling Frost... how?" Gabriel asked with a skeptical eyebrow.

"I've been with the boss when the call comes in. Hell... a lot of us have been since well... you know... new ladies, man." The captain gave him a sheepish smile. He withered under Gabriel's hard glare. His eyes flickered at the beamer. "Look... have I given you enough not to be shot?"

"That remains to be seen."

* * *

Gabriel irritably tapped his pencil as he reviewed his notes, scribbling little arrows between names to make the connections. "Takacy gets girls on hyped up charges in Atlanta... normally waifs off the street... sometimes middle-class women... occasionally bags a noblewoman...," he muttered as he drew a line upwards to where he had Anderson's name. "Anderson takes women that Takacy sends up to him for breeding and sale to local populace... or for sale to raiders at hefty prices... which he then uses to pay Takacy?" He threw down his pencil and rubbed his eyes. "Fuck me, I'm missing something here...," he breathed as he leaned back in his chair.

"You're forgetting that someone has to levy charges against the women to begin with," Coleton pointed out as he came over to the table and passed a mug of coffee to Gabriel. Then he sat down alongside Lincoln who was comparing notes with Gabriel. "Down in Atlanta," Coleton persisted. "You have to have a D.A. to prosecute."

"Not too hard in the Theocracy," Lincoln added, leaning back and stretching, the muscles in his ebony arms rippling. He then ran his hands back over his bald head as he leaned forward. "No shortage of attorneys down there thinking they're doing the Lord's work."

Gabriel snagged his notebook out of his pack and flipped it open to consult what he'd written down in Atlanta. "Ladd from the Spences was new... he set up Lucy during the

Consortium's trial to give him a slam dunk in the Theocracy trial." He trailed his pencil down the list. "They had a standard go-to guy up until Ladd."

"Rumor on the street has it that Ladd knew which way the wind was blowing when Eddie got sent up," Coleton said. Then he shrugged. "He didn't have to win that trial. There was no way for him to win it, not up against you, Deliverer, and Lucas Wolverton. Y'all had a solid case to the point that the trial was just a formality. You could've beamed him on capture and no one in New Eden of Geneva would've batted an eye."

"You know a lot about that case," Lincoln said with a smirk.

"Helps that I gathered evidence on this end of it," Coleton admitted.

"It is pretty convenient that Ladd got hired on by the Theocracy courts just after Eddie was executed and that his first trial was Lucy...," Gabriel thought out loud. "Takacy and Ladd were pretty chummy at the trial."

"So, you have two money trails here," Coleton pointed out, using a pencil to draw his own line to Ladd's name. He then stroked his black goatee as he thought things through out loud. "Takacy has Ladd in his pocket, obviously. Anderson is getting paid by the raiders, who use the gold to occasionally pay for girls in Atlanta, and that's it?" He shook his head. "No, there's got to be a money trail between Anderson and Takacy to go with the connection that you already have."

"Takacy has to be on the take from Anderson," Gabriel said. "It's the only explanation for why he'd be doing this to begin with."

"Hell, I can get that information for you in a half hour with a quick radiophone call to Atlanta," Coleton said with a dismissive wave of his hand as he got up from his chair and walked out of the room.

He returned twenty-five minutes later, grinning broadly and holding a few pages. He tossed them onto the table between Gabriel and Lincoln. "You were right on the hunch. Takacy has a steady stream of gold from Anderson labeled as 'reelection contributions,' and Ladd was hired directly by

Takacy with a sizable signing bonus when he became a D.A. for the court system. It's like I keep telling you regular Jaegers—just follow the damn money trail."

"Fucking hell...," Lincoln gasped, looking over the records. "And this goes back, what, ten years? How'd he keep it quiet for so long?"

"Small time donations, even ones labeled like this that are above the norms for a standard judge reelection campaign, don't trigger with the banks," Coleton explained. "So, unless y'all have a smoking gun like you do here." He spread his hands, shrugged, and shook his head. "Then there's no way to know it's there. Political corruption runs rampant everywhere so it's easy to obfuscate."

"Why Lucy, then?" Gabriel wondered out loud.

"Why not, man?" Lincoln was grim. "She's just another Theocratic girl caught up by events. I'm willing to bet you good money that they didn't expect a Jaeger to pop in at the last minute to see what they were up to."

"Had you been even fifteen minutes later to her trial, Gabe, we wouldn't have known anything," Coleton said. "Now we have this huge case blown open... thanks to you."

"Doesn't make me feel any better with Lucy in iSlave status." Gabriel muttered. "But, it's a start. Let's call this in to New Eden, get the evidence logged, and then get out to the Michaelson estate. Lucy will be thrilled to hear that we've made progress."

"We're also going to need to make house calls to every major house up and down the west coast of the Theocracy," Lincoln added, "before we check on your girl. If I know one thing, it is that when Wasteland raiders lose an airship, there's usually a big attack on the borders as they try to make up for the loss."

"Perfect... that's just all we need right now," Gabriel spat.

CHAPTER 11

Sticking with her set schedule, Lucy got up at the morning's first light. She took care of her personal business and hygiene before dressing in the very skimpy maid's outfit that Deacon required her to wear. It was a black and white frilly maid's dress in which the hem was high enough to leave little to the imagination and cut low enough to give support to her breasts while also leaving them exposed. It had been humiliating at first, but once she noticed that she was dressed just like every other house slave at the Michaelson estate, save for maybe the pair of favored pair of vSlaves that Deacon owned, that feeling soon passed. Once she was in the dress and hose, she put the lacy black and white choker into place over her iron collar, and then affixed the little maid's cap into her hair before applying her simple makeup.

Once in her 'uniform,' she left her small quarters in the attic level of the estate that was no bigger than the conjugal cell in Atlanta where she and Gabe had made love. It had the basic necessities and that was it—a corner shower stall and toilet, a sink right next to it, a single dresser with the different outfits that Deacon would want her to wear, and her bed. It was more furnished and private than her cell, so she couldn't complain about the upgrade.

Exiting the quarters, she followed the same path as she had for the last couple of months—down the narrow hall that ran under the peak beam of the estate to the wrought iron spiraling staircase that led down into the servant's wing.

She went down the four floors into the basement level, where one of her fellow maids was already serving breakfast for the entire staff—eggs, toast, sausage, water, and some juice. Lucy smiled and thanked her before wolfing down her meal and departing.

As much as she would've preferred to savor the meal, she quickly learned that there was no rest for a slave maid. If she ever regained her status as a prominent member of the aristocracy again, she'd make it a point to treat the house slaves with a bit more dignity and compassion. Their job was not an easy one.

Lucy set about her morning task, which was to report to the main kitchen directly above them, one floor up, and retrieve the tray of food that consisted of the family's breakfast and the most current newssheet.

RIGGING AIRSHIP *JAMESON'S REVENGE* GOES OFF THE RADAR. CHEYENNE SUSPECTED. *CONSORTIUM GOLD* TO BE DISPATCHED AT WEEK'S END.

Once upon a time, she would've been scared witless at the mention of the infamous air pirate, but today she could care less. Her life was much simpler now. With the large silver serving tray in her hands, she was allowed out to the main hallways where she would be in full view of the family and any guests they might have.

A quick stroll down the spacious open hallway, with its multiple works of art lining the walls and a maroon carpet that ran its length, and Lucy was at the massive dining room. The Michaelson family was now coming in, having just arose maybe a few minutes before she got there. The elder Michaelsons, seated side by side at the head of the table, were served their breakfast first. Lucy placed the massive tray down on a nearby tripod holder, lifted the cover to place to one side, and served them their respective plates first. Then it was Deacon's turn as the official head and manager of the house, along with the woman he was currently considering as a marriage match.

"Thank you, Lucy," Deacon said in his even tone as always, looking at her and admiring her semi-nude body with a nod of approval.

When she began her servitude with him, she blushed furiously under his gaze, but now she took it all in stride. She smiled brightly at him as she carried on her duties.

"Dear," the brunette, a girl named Suzie, said with a pointed look at Deacon by her side, "I really wish that you wouldn't look at the help in front of me like that."

"Why not?" Deacon asked playfully. "She's an attractive woman who I happen to own for the next ten years," he pointed out while giving his girlfriend with an equally pointed stare. "I could go even further, as is my right within the terms of her contract, to bend her, or any of my maids, over the table here and screw her while the family partakes of breakfast. Lucky for you, however, I treat my staff with far more dignity than that, regardless of what their original contract states."

To emphasize his point further, Deacon reached over to Lucy, up under her skirt, and cupped her sex. Lucy froze, not sure if she liked that he was doing that, and then quickly realizing that she didn't really have a choice in the matter. By law, he *could* bend her over the table right now and take her.

This was actually the first time he'd touched her. She had been feeling needy and hadn't had any intimate contact since Gabriel on her last rights night. A few months ago, she was sitting just like Deacon's suitress at a table, facing a marriage prospect, and now here she was a lowly slave. But, that was not what she found peculiar. It was odd because she felt freer now than she ever had. Gone were the days of worrying about goodness and propriety. Now, she just had to know what to do, and didn't have to think about whether she was upsetting any particular member of society. Now, she only had one person to please, and that was the man who was now fondling her, while having a stern talk to his potential betrothed. It was a freer life, but bizarre in its own way.

She lost track of the argument that erupted between Deacon and his girlfriend, instead focusing on the desire welling up inside her and her inclination to keep as straight a face as possible. It didn't help that Deacon kept glancing at her body, while giving her mound a squeeze, just to prove a point to Suzie. Lucy closed her eyes, took deep, calming breaths through her nose, and bit her lower lip to keep her passion in check.

"Thank you, Lucy," Deacon said finally by way of dismissal, taking his hand away and flicking it in her direction.

Blushing furiously, Lucy managed a polite curtsey before quickly gathering the serving tray and hustling out of the room as fast as her legs could take her. Rushing back down the hallway and into the kitchen, Lucy unceremoniously dumped the tray into the nearest wash basin before heading back down the stairs into the safety of a bathroom. Locking the door behind her, she planted herself over the simple sink and took more calming breaths to calm her nerves and drive her elevated passion down a few notches. Off in the distance, she heard the ring of an incoming call, but ignored it as her duties lay in serving and cleaning, not answering the radio telephones.

She took a few minutes in the bathroom to compose herself so that she'd be presentable as she carried out her duties for the rest of the day. After splashing some water over her flushed face and chest and drying herself off, she slid a hand down her black panties to confirm what she already knew—she was wet, all because of her master's attention. Knowing that she didn't have enough time to rush back up to her quarters to change, Lucy dried herself off with some tissue, flushed it, and then checked herself out in the mirror to ensure that she was presentable once again. Part of her felt guilty that Deacon... Lord Michaelson... could make her feel this way, but the reality was that Gabriel was her past and this was her future... for the next ten years, anyway.

There wasn't much time to lose as the entire household would be busy today with preparations for the Michaelsons' end of summer gala. She would just have to take care of herself in her quarters later, another activity that she would've never have done when she was a part of the prim and proper society above.

"Lucy!" Deacon's sharp yell echoed through the serving corridors. She jerked upright at her master's call. How long had she been in there? "Get your hind end back out here at once!"

Thankfully, she was already in motion just from hearing her name being called. She hastened back out into the main hall where Deacon waited impatiently with crossed arms and a stern look.

"Yes, Master," she said with a bow of her head and a deep curtsey.

"I have a special VIP guest coming for the party tonight who just called. You're excused from gala preparations for the day. I want you to get the primary guest suite ready and then stand by in there until I come for you. *You* are going to be his entertainment for the day, and this evening, you're to be at the front door with me to take guests' hats and coats."

Bowing her head again despite the heat rising to her face, Lucy managed another curtsey, albeit a shaky one.

"Y-Yes, Master," she acknowledged morosely.

This was something new. She'd never been dictated to entertain any of his guests before and if the primary suite was to be used then there was no doubt in her mind as to what kind of 'entertainment' she'd be required to do. She'd heard the other maids talk.

"Off with you, then. They will be here a little after noon before the main festivities begin. This means you do not have much time."

"Yes, Master." Lucy repeated as she hustled off to her new duty for the day while her heart thudded in her chest with fear and uncertainty.

***

Gabriel's brass armor-encased hand curled into a fist before he banged on the front doors to the estate. A semi-nude maid opened it a few moments later and looked up at him with wide eyes in full Jaeger armor. This was not quite the occasion to see such an outfit and he knew it.

"Jaeger Messenger here for Deacon Michaelson," his mechanical voice came out of his helmet. Without a word, the now pale-faced maid rushed off as fast as her legs would carry her. Gabriel chuckled to himself while he waited. A Jaeger showing up would be cause for alarm on any given day. Having one show up in armor could potentially cause a panic.

A moment later, Deacon appeared at the door with crossed arms and an arched eyebrow. "A bit early for theatrics, don't you think?"

Gabriel shrugged, the servos in his arms and shoulders whining a bit in the process. "What do you want? Full dress uniform? I've helped down a raider airship recently and then I've been out warning estates in the area, all the from Atlanta to the coast about possible reprisal attacks. I had at least a dozen of noble houses to get to *before* yours, so I opted for the armor with flight package," he said as he removed his helmet. Gabriel shook his head to let his hair out, as it was hot and stifling inside all that brass. "I've been at this for a good couple of weeks now," he added, sounding as weary as felt.

"You're doing this house by house?" Worry and concern crossed Deacon's face as he waved Gabriel in. "Is there something going on that I need to be aware of?" he asked, making a pointed look at the huge beamer cannon that made up the entire left arm of Gabriel's armor. The cannon was so over-the-top it made him look like another worldly being.

"Hopefully not, but we're treating it as something to notify the populace about, anyway," Gabriel said as he followed Deacon inside, his brass armor clanging and his heavy footsteps making soft thuds in the rugs. "Rumors have been flying around about raiders out of the Wastelands pushing farther inland after Cheyenne's attack north of Atlanta a few months back. Since then, more girls have gone missing out of New Mobile, a rigging airship has gone dark, and skirmishes have all increased all around. Then we captured that one airship up north and now we're bracing for reprisal attacks. It's like they all smell blood in the water and everyone is itching to get a bite. One of the rumors state that they're going to go for a major attack so the Consortium has me, Emancipator, and a few others out west here to warn everyone and to tell them to get their defenses up and running. The Dixie Air Corps has their forces mobilized and out on patrol, just in case."

"Sounds like you're doing everything that you can, then," Deacon said as they walked up the grand staircase in the middle of the entry hall to the second floor. He flagged down his butler and relayed instructions to get the house airships on alert and then continued on with Gabriel. Deacon motioned to the right down one hall that led to the eastern wing. "So now you can relax and spend some time with your girlfriend."

Gabriel shot him a dirty look through the eye visor. "She's not my girlfriend. She's... your slave," he said, unable to hide his irritation.

"Oh, please, I heard the wistfulness in your voice when you called me to buy her. I could picture the glazed look in your eye every time I said her name." Deacon chuckled. "Is that why you took her case on?" he asked, his voice becoming somber. "To get your ex back?"

"I dunno," Gabriel admitted, blowing out a long breath. "Part of me wanted to see if she remembered and to see if the girl I knew was still in there. Part of me cheered when I saw the Spences finally take a fall and I felt some measure of justification when I'd heard that she'd been implicated along with her brother."

"But...," Deacon gently prodded.

"But," Gabriel conceded with a sigh, "when I saw her through the interrogation mirror, a lump caught in my throat as I saw the same, sweet, innocent girl that I'd known and I got protective of her all over again. I was ready to be her entire world back when the McKibben name meant something around here and I quickly became the role of her protector once again. I changed my stance at once to be her advocate when I heard that she had none. When questioning her, I concluded that she was as much a victim in all of this, if not more so, as my family had been."

"How is your case going?"

"I have enough to put it to the Consortium to make Takacy and Anderson look shifty, but not altogether guilty." Gabriel shook his head. "I need just a little bit more in order to get them into an interrogation facility and throw the book at them."

"Mm-hm," Deacon nodded non-committal and then looked over at his friend. "When are you going to tell her?" he asked with a pointed look.

"About her case? As soon as I can."

"Not that. About *why* you took her case."

"I don't know... it was a long time ago... it's not like it matters much anyway."

"Well, here's your chance to come clean since confession is good for the soul," Deacon said with a sly grin as he stopped at the VIP room, opening the door. "You can get out of your armor here, get cleaned up, relax, and stay here until the gala tonight. My slave maid will see to your *every* need," he said and waggled his eyebrows suggestively.

CHAPTER 12

"Gabriel!" Lucy bolted upright in the bed, her hands shooting straight to her mouth in shock. She couldn't believe that Deacon had arranged this, and the extent of her excited outburst surprised her as well.

She slid off the bed as fast as she could, swallowing hard as she tried to gain some composure. "My apologies, Master, for my indiscretion." She curtsied low, bowed her head and looked between Deacon and Gabriel.

Deacon waved it off. "Considering that you didn't jump immediately into his arms like I half expected you to, I guess we can skip the flogging this time... unless *you* want to do that, Gabe." He winked with a wolfish grin. "Have fun you two."

"Wait! Master! This... this is the VIP?" Lucy couldn't help but blurt out.

"Surprise!" Deacon laughed as he closed the door behind him. "Have fun until the gala!"

Lucy and Gabriel stood there, staring at each other for an awkward moment and then Lucy gave in to her first impulse and rushed over to him to give him a big hug, armor and all. "I've missed you!"

"Same here," Gabriel said, now grinning like the cat who ate the canary. "Let me get out of this first?" He took off his helmet and handed it to her. Lucy placed it on a nearby chest of drawers as he shuffled over to the side of the door. He engaged the side locks of his suit that immobilized the legs from the waist down. Then he twisted on two valves on either shoulder and the whole chest assembly hydraulics hissed as they rose upward. The arms of the suit lifted over his head as if he were trying to take flight. Then he grabbed two handholds that came out from the inside of the suit and lifted his entire body up and out of the armor like he was a gymnast.

"Ta-dah," he said with a mock flourish of his arms out to either side.

Lucy let off a light laugh at his silliness before rushing back into his arms. It felt good to be in his embrace once again and this time she couldn't resist the urge to raise up and plant a full kiss on his lips. "I've missed you," she said again.

"I've missed you, too," he murmured in between kisses.

She smiled playfully, wrinkling her nose as she pushed back from him. "As much as I'd like to continue this, first things first, oh high and mighty VIP. You need a shower. You stink of sweat." She took him by the hand and led him to the adjoining bathroom. "We'll have to get laundry done on your clothes after we're done with you."

"To be fair, I've been in my armor nearly non-stop for two weeks now," Gabriel snickered, matching her smile. "I've barely had time to sleep, let alone catch a decent shower. But don't worry about clothes—my uniform is in the armor's travel pack."

"Excuses, excuses...," she replied, moving over to the large stand-up glass shower that had a tile base so that it could double as an enclosed luxury tub. Lucy opened the door and bent over to manipulate the levers and knobs to turn on the water. She watched it gush down like a waterfall until it reached just the right temperature. When she stood up and turned, she caught Gabriel admiring the view of her posterior.

"Get a good look?" she asked, batting her eyelashes.

"Yes, thank you," Gabriel admitted, his smile even broader now. "I've always loved how the Michaelsons dressed their maids up, but you certainly do the outfit justice."

"I've been told by a certain Jaeger that I look even better without it on," she smiled at him, hooking her arms through the shoulder straps of her uniform and slipped it off. The skimpy dress fell to the floor, followed by her shoes, panties, garters, and hose shortly thereafter

Gabriel feigned heartbreak. "You've been seeing another Jaeger behind my back? I'm devastated," he said with a dramatic sigh. "I must find him and kill him."

"I wouldn't worry," Lucy quipped, stepping up to him and unbuttoning his shirt. "He's just some blowhard advocate out of Atlanta. Hardly worth your time." She gave him a wink as she undressed him. When she got him out of his boots and pants, she saw just how much he desired her. "In a little bit," she promised, kissing the head of his cock before rising up and leading him into the shower.

He arched an eyebrow. "Coming in with me, are you?"

"Well, this is a full-service establishment, and my Master did order me to give you the best VIP treatment available before his gala tonight." Lucy closed the door behind them and proceeded to rinse him down before pumping a lever that let out a spray of foam soap. Lucy worked it up and down his body, her hands tracing over his powerful muscles, broad shoulders, and toned legs. When she was done scrubbing him down and rinsing them off, she was on her knees again in front of him. She shuffled forward and tentatively kissed the head of his cock again before taking it slowly into her mouth.

Gabriel groaned with pleasure, bracing his hands on the walls on either side of him for support. "Dear God... you didn't do that in Atlanta," he noted.

"Been talking with the girls here recently," Lucy told him after she pulled back. "Considering most of them are pleasure vSlaves, they have a lot of tips to give." She leaned in, closed her eyes, and took him back into her mouth, going farther down his shaft this time.

She could feel him watching her while she sucked him off. Her pretty pink lips traveled up and down his length as she softly sucked every time she drew back.

Suddenly, he hissed, "No teeth! No teeth! Open up more!" he begged her, sounding pained.

She immediately drew back and let him go. "Sorry! Are you okay?"

"I will be, just relax your mouth to keep those pearly whites of yours away," he suggested.

She did so and he moaned again with pleasure. "That's more like it." He winced when she accidentally nipped him again and he put a stop to it. "I think that I want you on the bed now," he said, reaching behind her and turning off the water.

"I'll get better, I promise," Lucy said as she stood and fetched a towel.

"I'm sure you will and I'll be more than happy to let you practice," Gabriel said as he stepped out of the shower with her and let her gently dry him off, her playful eyes teasing him.

97

"But we only have so long until we need to be dressed and ready for Deak's party tonight," He added. He picked up her dainty frame and carried her back out to the bed in the suite, gently placing her down. "Hmm... much more comfortable than the last bed we were in."

"Yes, much," she agreed, parting her legs for him.

Gabriel's hand slid around to cup her now smooth mound. Lucy moaned passionately in response. She lifted her hips up to meet his touch. "Shaved now?" he asked.

"Required...," she breathed, "since I'm owned now."

"I kinda liked your strawberry blonde curls," he murmured as he started kissing the side of her head down to her neck. He stopped when his lips met the metal collar. "These damn things always get in the way."

"Just kiss me," Lucy whimpered.

He followed her orders and planted his lips onto hers as she brought her delicate hands up to frame his chiseled face. His finger dipped into her sex and she squealed into his mouth. Gabriel continued kissing her while slowly moving his finger in and out of her, dragging his finger up and down the front wall of her pussy. Lucy let out quick, tiny moans every time his finger pulled out of her, lifting her hips to meet his next push of his finger back into her. Fire radiated out from her loins and she shuddered under his touch. She reached down and stroked him to hardness as their bodies moved next to each other.

Suddenly, Lucy was overcome with the desire to try something else that the other maids had talked about, so she gently pushed on his shoulder to roll him onto his back. He gave her a questioning look and she smiled as she slid one leg up and over him to straddle his hips. Gabriel caught on quickly and gently raised her up while she positioned his cock just right so that she could ease down onto him. Lucy sighed with pleasure as she felt his cock fill her up once again. She arched her back as she tentatively moved up and down. Then she felt his hands on her hips, guiding her into a grinding motion that made her clit ground down against his pubis. "Oh my God...," she moaned, overwhelmed by the intense sensation.

Gabriel smiled up at her, clearly enjoying the view from

where he lay. As she moved her hips back and forth, he moved one hand around to rest against her abdomen. She looked down at him, wondering what he was up to. His smile turned wicked as he then proceeded to brush his thumb back and forth across her clit. Lucy moaned in pleasure as tiny electrodes of ecstasy ripped through her, tingling all the way down her extremities.

Moments later, she bucked hard on top of him as the orgasm pulsed through her body unexpectedly. She placed her hands down onto his hard, muscular chest to brace herself as she started quivering violently on top of him. Her legs shuddered and jerked on their own accord. Her arms vibrated hard and felt like they'd turned to rubber. Lucy's mouth was locked in an open *O* as her entire world turned white. She felt herself fall and Gabriel was there to catch her in his powerful arms, wrapping her up and holding her close to his chest.

She moaned pathetically as her body trembled, intermittently fluttering around him. "Oh... God...," she gurgled.

"And we're not even done yet...." Gabriel gave her a mischievous look as he rolled them in the bed until she was underneath him.

Locking eyes with Gabriel, Lucy braced her arms against his shoulders and lifted her legs up as he slowly thrust into her.

"Ahhhhhh!" she gasped, arching her body into her as his cock pushed into her now sensitive pussy. Her whole body shuddered again as he made slow, deliberate thrusts. His hand came up to cup her breast, his thumb now brushing back and forth across her nipple, teasing the already hard nub.

Part of Lucy's mind thought back to what he'd said when they met in Atlanta about having the ability to pleasure a woman with just his thumb. It certainly held up to the test thus far. When she reached her peak again, Gabriel was right there with her as he let out a long, low groan. His seed flooded into her as their sweaty bodies trembled and gyrated together. Her body folded, her thighs gripped his sides, and her pussy squeezed and released his cock as it throbbed inside of her endlessly. Once it was all over, they collapsed together in a tangle of limbs, bodies humming, and neither saying anything as the luxuriated in the moment.

After a while, Lucy shifted uncomfortably next to him. There was one question that had been gnawing at her since he'd arrived. "What did he mean earlier when he asked you when you were going to tell me something?"

"Hm?" Gabriel asked. Lucy realized he'd started to doze off. "Him? Who? What?" Gabriel asked.

"Master Michaelson… about why you took my case and you said something about a long time ago. What was it?" she asked, raising up to look him in the face. Gabriel squirmed, his face betraying his emotions. "You knew it was me before you took my case, didn't you?"

From the look on his face, Lucy could tell that he'd been discovered. "Yeah," he said softly, "I knew it was you… I was pulled out of a lecture that I was giving at the academy and handed your dossier."

"And you took my case anyway? Even after you'd left me? Why?" Lucy demanded, her eyes now intently on him.

"I didn't leave you, dammit! I was forced out of the Theocracy because your family ruined my family ten years ago, okay?" Gabriel said harshly. "The Carmichaels were not your family's first victims. Far from it, in fact. They'd pulled the same scam on us. We built small naval gunships, both water and air, out of the Grenada and Winona area over by the bay."

Lucy frowned. "Spence Military Industries owns those areas now."

Gabriel shot her a sour look as he kicked his feet off the bed. "Used to be MMI—McKibben Military Industries." He shook his head, looking disgusted. "You remember when I was betrothed to you and was supposed to be your husband and protector? I took that role seriously. We only had a few dates and I respected your brother's insistence that you wanted to remain pure until the wedding."

"I never said that!" Lucy couldn't believe what she was hearing.

"I figured as much," Gabriel said and blew out a long breath. "Anyway, you may remember that my sister was also betrothed to Eddie back when he was just out of university school and she was out of high school. It was our parents' way of maintaining strong ties between the families. The marriage arrangement fell through because her accounts had been sucked dry... by your brother. Sound familiar now? Your father then accused me of plotting the same thing against you and broke off the betrothal, but never paid back the bride price that we'd already paid out."

His eyes settled back onto her and she could see the accusation behind them. "Your father then blackmailed my parents and forced them into servitude in Taylorsville. My sister committed suicide because she was facing a future as a slave to be sold off to the Wastelands."

"What? No!" Lucy gasped in horror. "What'd you do?"

"I fled the country, despite wanting to take the last of our airships up north to get my family back." Gabriel gestured out the door. "Deak and his family took me in until I could get passage out of the country."

Lucy's heart was pounding in her chest. She just stared at him, aghast. "So, how does *he* owe *you*?"

"I saved him and his family by giving him all of my house assets that I had access to. The west coast of the Theocracy is always under attack from raiders. Before your father and brother could scoop up all my family's assets, I'd hijacked several of our gunboats and static defenses and transferred the titles over to the Michaelsons and rigged the paperwork to make it look like legitimate transfers and was able to back it up to local authorities. Just in time, too, as a raid happened shortly thereafter. The Michaelsons were able to defend all of their assets and flourish as a result. Deak said that he owed me big time for saving their family even though I wasn't able to save my own."

Wiping the tears from her eyes, Lucy pressed on. "And your parents?"

Gabriel shook his head and closed his eyes. A pained expression spread across his face. "I think I'm done with the history lesson for now."

Another thought occurred to her. "Then why on earth did you take my case?" she asked, her voice now taking on a sharp edge. "Was it to see me suffer? Was it not enough to see my brother executed?"

101

"You know what?" Gabriel snapped right back as he stood up. "Believe it or not, no. After all these years, I still harbored some fondness for you and I was actually grateful that you hadn't been corrupted like all the men in your family. I tried recusing myself from the case, but my boss insisted. Then I thought maybe I was just fulfilling my oath as a Jaeger to protect and serve the innocents and to keep a balanced playing field for you." He sighed. "Doesn't matter now."

"You should've told me from the beginning what had happened to you!" Lucy said, unable to keep her voice from raising.

Gabriel opened his arms in askance. "Would it have made a difference, or would you have asked for another Jaeger to defend you? Keep in mind that another Jaeger probably wouldn't have dropped everything to come defend you at your Theocracy trial, there, princess."

"That's not the point!" Lucy was on her feet.

Slave or no, she was going to get this out, damn the consequences. She came around the bed and jabbed her finger right into the middle of his chest. "*You* harbored this information from me all of this time! At one point, you even said that you loved me. You should have let me know instead of keeping me in the dark all this time! Instead, you acted just like the spoiled, arrogant jerk that you were when you were younger!"

He cocked his head at that. "Spoiled?" He harrumphed. "That's rich, coming from you. You know, it could be argued here that you failed to speak up when you had the chance."

"No!" she jabbed her finger into his chest, pushed him away, and then headed for the door. "Don't you dare go all lawyering on me now, *Mr.* McKibben!" She threw open the door.

"Don't you need this?" Gabriel asked, holding up her skimpy maid's uniform.

"Oh, keep it! It's not like I have anything to hide anymore, unlike certain Jaegers that I know!" she yelled, slamming the door behind her and stalking up to her room to get a replacement uniform.

CHAPTER 13

As it turned out for Lucy, most of the people in the mansion heard her fight with Gabriel. Per her assigned duties from earlier, Deacon had her out collecting hats, overcoats, shawls, and whatever else guests had on as they arrived for the gala. In the back courtyard, the band was in full swing. The entire estate was lit up with the soft glow of electric lanterns as night started to settle in. Clockworks milled about with trays of hour d'oeuvres and glasses of wine and champagne.

Lucy had to fight the urge to run. While guests poured in, she saw many that she recognized. Most of them looked down at her with open disdain on their faces, though they were quick to smile for Deacon as he received them, complimenting him on his bold choice to take in a criminal to rehabilitate. Her face burned with shame at each comment, but she managed to keep a civil tongue.

"Baroness Carmichael," Deacon said, greeting the platinum blonde warmly as she walked in on the arm of a handsome businessman in a neatly tailored suit. The name alone got Lucy's attention as she stood by to receive whatever overgarments her master's guests might bring. She gasped when she saw the happy couple now coming in the doorway. She supposed it was inevitable that once again she'd be reminded about why she fell from grace in the first place.

Deacon regarded the man as he shook hands with him. "You must be Charity's new husband. I do apologize, but I missed the name."

"Lucas Wolverton!" Lucy blurted out as the memories of her arrest and interrogation by the Consortium official returned, causing the three of them to look at her. She blushed and dropped her head in embarrassment. "My apologies... sir."

Deacon gave her a puzzled look and then recovered. "*Baron*, to you," he said crossly. "After all, he did marry into the Carmichael fortune. And your outbursts today...."

"Please, relax," Lucas said with a charming smile as he waved it off. "I'm an accountant with the Consortium first, and a newly married Theocracy noble second." He stepped in and took Lucy's hand, dipping down to brush her knuckles with his lips as if she were still a noblewoman. "Lady Spence, it is good to see you again although I wish it were under better circumstances," he said before stepping back to his wife's side.

Lucy was floored by his display of respect and was now blushing for an entirely different reason. It was the first time that anyone other than Gabriel had treated her like a lady. "Umm... thank you... sir."

At least he wasn't kicking my parlor door down this time, she thought.

"That's not necessary, you know," Deacon pointed out. "While I do appreciate the gesture, she is still an iSlave, after all."

"As far as the Theocracy is concerned, sure," Lucas admitted. "However, from what I understand, her case is still under investigation and review at the Consortium level. Therefore, we'll treat her how her birthright entails, regardless of the collar she wears or the clothes...," he looked Lucy up and down, "or lack thereof, that she wears."

"It is?" Lucy blinked.

Gabriel hadn't told her that. Then again, they did have that fight before he had a chance to.

"Of course," Deacon smiled as he shifted his gaze back to Charity. "I wasn't expecting you here after all that went on a couple months back, Lady Carmichael."

Charity smiled and hugged her husband's arm. "We're on our way back home from our honeymoon since it was already paid for. We didn't want all that planning and money to go to waste."

"That, and the Consortium owes me a ton of back leave," Lucas added. "We're due to return to Elysium at the end of the week on the *Consortium Gold*. Even though we don't have time to settle in very much until we have to be out to Vegaston on business."

"Just watch out for the Angel while you're out there—I hear he's worse than all the raiders in the Wastelands put together." Deacon let out a polite laugh and waved them on. "It's good to have you both here. We'll have to talk later. I'd

104

love to know the details. In the meantime, welcome to the gala. Please, enjoy yourselves."

Lucy couldn't help but watch the couple as they moved into the manor, arm in arm, looking totally in love. The last time she had seen them, Charity was wearing the black felt collar of a vSlave, but now it was gone from her neck. Did Mr. Wolverton release her from her contract?

With her hand absently drifting up to her own collar, Lucy felt the cold metal as if it had just been put on her for the first time. She'd criticized and was demeaning to Charity then. Now, Lucy was the slave, and not of the voluntary variety, either. It was taught that one's sins came back to haunt them and maybe this was Lucy's punishment for being so cruel to Charity.

"Pay attention, Lucy!" Deacon hissed at her, snapping her out of her thoughts.

Lucy jerked to attention and put her eyes forward as she saw the next couple of nobles walking up the path. It was none other than Lord Edward Vickers and his young wife, Lady Feckla Vickers. The Vickers were one of the more powerful families in Atlanta and thus very well connected.

"My, my, my," Feckla said as she eyed Lucy. "Lucy Spence, naked and in a slave collar." She gave a disapproving *tsk*. "My how your family has crumbled," she added while her husband greeted and made small talk with Deacon.

Lucy bowed her head and lowered her gaze. "Lady Vickers," she said formally with a curtsy as etiquette required. This was now beyond humiliating as the Vickers had been the third call she'd made when arrested right after her father and Gabriel. The Vickers had declined to help, despite their families' connections.

Feckla gave a cruel smile, reaching out to lift Lucy's chin. Lucy was close enough to see the pale streak of blonde highlights in the woman's otherwise chestnut brown hair; the style was supposedly to be all the rage this season. "Oh, how the high and mighty Spences have fallen, with one of their daughters wearing iron." She shook her head as if scolding a temperamental child. "Your father must be very proud."

"I wouldn't know, m'lady," Lucy said evenly and formally. "He has declined to speak to me since he kicked me out."

He also declined to show up tonight, thank the Lord.
Lucy wasn't sure if she could handle that embarrassment.

"For good reason, I'd imagine." She took her shawl off and handed it to Lucy as if holding out a piece of garbage. "Do take care of this for me, will you, dear? Thank you and bless your heart," she added piously as she took her husband's arm and entered the manor.

Her face burning with shame, Lucy deposited the shawl in the nearby closet before returning to Deacon's side. "Sorry about that. I'd thought to have you back inside by the time the Vickers came since they're usually fashionably late. Now the assholes decide to show up on time."

She managed a small smile. "Thank you, Master." Indeed, the line of guests was thinning considerably now that the festivities were about to begin.

After a few more guests were greeted, Deacon couldn't hide the surprise on his face at the last man in line who stepped up to be received. "Overseer Anderson, this is... unexpected. I haven't seen you since the auction in Atlanta."

"Yes," Clark Anderson confirmed coolly, "when you bought the woman I'd intended on getting right out from underneath of me."

"Really?" Gabriel couldn't help but say, as he stepped up next to Lucy so quietly that it made her jump. She did a double take and saw that he was in his dress uniform now. Ice was evident in his voice. "And why would a prison overseer of one of those breeder farms want to purchase anyone from open auction when you just get inmates assigned to your facility at a regular basis?"

"Ah, yes, the Jaeger who kept Miss Spence from me in the first place," Anderson said, his gaze dropping the temperature around them by several degrees. "You should learn your place among your betters, boy, and stop meddling in Theocracy affairs."

"Deak?" Gabriel mused, "did it sound like Overseer Anderson just threatened a Consortium Jaeger?"

"One could certainly interpret it that way," Deacon said with a solemn nod.

When he realized the overstep on his part, Anderson's eyebrow's shot up for a mere instant before dropping back into his cool, aloof demeanor. "I just meant that you should concern yourself with more pressing matters, like bandits in the Wastelands, for example." Before Gabriel could respond, Anderson turned his attention back to Deacon. "Now, you have repeatedly ignored my requests to buy your new slave from you."

"No, I've just given it all the consideration it's due." Deacon shook his head. "The answer was no two months ago, and it was no a month ago, and it is still no now." He smiled thinly. "Welcome to my family's gala, I do hope that you'll enjoy yourself."

Anderson stiffened Deacon's dismissal and managed a curt nod before moving on. He tossed his cloak and top hat at the nearest startled maid without looking her way. The maid scrambled to catch it and hastened the garments off to the cloak room. Gabriel and Deacon watched him disappear into the crowd.

"He's been asking to buy Lucy off you since the auction?" Gabriel asked, leaning in to Deacon.

"Yeah," Deacon nodded, giving Gabriel a sideways glance. "She's been more trouble than she's worth just because of *him*."

"You owe me. Just keep her safe until I can get all of my evidence to free her."

"*You* keep her safe for tonight no matter if you two are fighting or not. As for me, I'm going to go get drunk and enjoy the company of my slaves and soon to be fiancé... maybe all at once...." Deacon cast another glance at Gabriel. "I swear to God, Gabe, after you free her we're even."

"Fine by me," Gabriel muttered as he took Lucy by the arm to keep her close by.

CHAPTER 14

"**W**ill you let me go?" Lucy hissed, twisting in Gabriel's grasp. "I'm still angry with you!"

"No," Gabriel responded in kind. "Not with Anderson here eyeing you. I don't trust the man."

"I can take care of myself!"

"And how's that been working for you?" Gabriel pulled her into a side hallway and pinned her up against the wall. He glanced around to make sure no one was paying attention before he leaned in close as if to neck with her. Lucy squirmed and his hand shot up to the other side of her neck to keep her still.

"Stop it! Just listen to me for a second! I didn't have a chance to tell you about your case because we got... umm... sidetracked."

"And whose fault is that?" she asked wryly although a touch of anger was still in her voice. It didn't help being in such close, intimate proximity to him yet again. Her loins shouted for her to jump on him.

"Look, Anderson's name has been coming up on all of Takacy's court records and on Takacy's financial records. They have a racket going on. On any given case, it's always a single lady who is forced by Theocracy law to either remain silent or defend herself without an advocate. Your case is the first one in years in which an advocate has shown up," he urgently explained. "On paper, it's all legit. But when you add it all up over time, it paints an ugly picture of what the Consortium forbids."

"Illegal slavery...." Lucy's eyes widened as she gasped. "They're... they're using the system to do it?"

"Much like what your family was doing. It's why we have so many Jaegers in theocratic nations around the world... especially in Dixie and New Zion," Gabriel confirmed. "They like to game the system to their advantage. Now, I'm going to keep a close eye on Anderson. If you can, since I'm sure he'll come near you again, see if you can get him to talk."

Lucy shuddered, not wanting to be anywhere near that man. "But, no court will believe what I have to say, not without my father saying so."

Gabriel pulled back and smiled at her. "No, *Theocratic* court will and it doesn't matter; your father doesn't have a say anymore since he disowned you. Deak does. He's your legal master and this is a Consortium matter now."

Glancing out at the party that was getting into full swing, Lucy felt uneasy. "What if he tries to grab me?"

"He'd be stupid to do so." Gabriel looked up as if beseeching the heavens. "Oh, please let him be that stupid. That'll make my job a whole lot easier and with less paperwork." He smiled at her and gave her a quick peck on the cheek. "Relax, you'll be fine. I'm here. Deak and his whole family are here. Hell, I even saw one of our Consortium accountants here who was at your brother's trial. You're covered."

"I hope that you're right about this."

***

It only took an hour before Anderson made his move toward Lucy. She was by the buffet table in the back courtyard clearing away empty dishes when he came up to her.

"Oh! Excuse me, sir," she'd turned and nearly ran into him, jostling the platters in her nervousness. "I didn't see you there, sir. Please forgive me."

"Hmm, no forgiveness is necessary, child," Anderson purred, his eyes roving over her entire body. His finger came up and flicked the underside of her metal collar. "I can make this disappear, you know."

Lucy didn't buy his act for a minute. She gave him the sweetest Dixie smile that she could muster, while inside she shuddered in revulsion at his touch. "That's very kind of you, sir, but I have to get these back to the kitchen."

He grabbed her by the arm as she went to move past him, pulling her close. "I'm serious. Just say the word and this collar is gone," he whispered into her ear.

"And what word would that be, sir?" Lucy asked hesitantly.

"I want you to be my wife."

Unable to help herself, she looked up at him. "Why? You

were going to have me thrown away into your breeder farm?"

He smiled down at her. "Oh, you are going to join me there, one way or another. Whether I buy you from Michaelson or find some other less legal way to do it, you *will* be mine. The daughter of Reverend Spence? Your family has helped me more though the years than they realize, with all the families they've ruined. With you by my side, I'd be in the perfect position to take over the last of their assets now that they've fallen from grace and are no longer helpful." His hand drifted down to her belly and she felt a wave of nausea creep up. He squeezed possessively. "And with a baby in here, an heir would be indisputable. So, just say that you'll be mine and you'll have your freedom back."

Lucy was in a near panic, but her eyes somehow detected Charity Carmichael... or to be precise, Charity Wolverton... in the crowd. Charity had become a slave to Mr. Wolverton to avoid being a slave to Lucy's brother. Lucy's free hand drifted up to her own collar to touch the metal. Would she really be free, or would she just trading one form of slavery for another? After all, how free would she be if she said yes?

She looked up at him, her defiance now showing. "No, thank you."

Anderson's face hardened as he jerked her once to get right into her face. "I will have you! One way or another!"

"You wouldn't dare do anything with two Consortium officials here!" she shot back, now yanking her arm free. She managed to keep a hold of the dishes and platters. "Good day, sir!"

"Fine," he said, grabbing her again. "Plan B it is."

Anderson reached into his inner jacket pocket, and pulled out a device that looked like a box with dials and a wire sticking out of the top. He pressed a button and spoke into it. "Do it now."

"Do what now?" Lucy asked, suddenly feeling fearful.

He smirked. "We have more guests coming to the party, my dear."

***

"What the hell is that?" Deacon observed as he peered up into the night sky. The deep, rumbling *whomp whomp whomp* sound of old airship propeller engines filled the air, preceding a dark shape that moved through the night sky.

Gabriel squinted and saw the Ice Star on Sand and Blood symbol on the huge ramshackle rudder. He swore under his breath.

"Oh, sure, *now*, they decide to fucking attack!" he whirled around, calling to the guests as he started running for the doors. "Raiders! Get out of here now!" Turning to Deacon he added, "Whoever doesn't get gone, get them inside and hole up."

"Where are you going?" Deacon demanded even as he drew his own beamer from under his blazer.

"To get my armor on and to call for backup, that's where!" Gabriel called over his shoulder. "Where's your house fleet, anyway?" He was met with Deacon's confused shrug.

He was up the grand staircase and in his suite in no time at all. Gabriel keyed the radio in his helmet as he jumped into his armor, grabbing the overhead hand holds to pull himself up before dropping his legs in.

"Emancipator! This is Messenger! Get yer ass up here to the Michaelson Estate, pronto! We're under attack by raiders!"

On the other end of the line, Jaeger Emancipator swore. "I'll be on my way, man. ETA twenty minutes," he said in his smooth, velvet voice that never lost its calm demeanor.

"Better make it ten—they're already hot and bearing those markings belonging to Auctor Frost that you told me about," Gabriel urged him, locking down the chest piece and then grabbing for his helmet. He slammed it down on top of his head and twisted slightly to the left, locking it into place. The armor whirred to life, now under his full control. Inside his left arm, he gripped the firing mechanism for his arm's Gatling gun. A single squeeze of the pressure grip got the barrels spinning around his forearm. All he had to do was jam his thumb down onto the trigger assembly for it to spit out white-hot death to anyone unlucky enough to be in its path. Now in his protective shell, Gabriel ran back out to the foyer, footsteps thundering in the hallway with each step.

111

***

Lucy was aghast as she was dragged along by the arm through the halls of the manor.

"You called raiders here?" she squeaked amid the commotion of guests and staff running this way and that, all trying to find cover or protection from the attack. "Just to get me?" There was beamer fire off to her left where Mr. Wolverton had upended a table, thrown Charity behind it, and started shooting at the party crashers.

"You failed to see reason, my dear," Anderson said harshly.

"But they'll capture or even kill people here!"

"And you could've avoided this had you just taken me up on my offer!" he snapped. "This impending bloodshed is on you! Not me!"

The *thump-thump* sound of cannons firing from overhead rumbled over the manor followed by a couple of explosions out front as some of the guests' steam and motor carriages were destroyed, preventing people from escaping. More cannon shots rang out, this time closer as the raider airship got near. More explosions. People screamed and cried out in terror as they ran every which way for cover.

Lucy tried to twist out of Anderson's grip to no avail. He kept a hold on her as solid as the iron collar she wore. "You can't do this! Let me go!" she protested.

"I've been doing this for years and it's all been arranged. After your master is dead, you go back to auction. Having 'saved' you from this vile raider attack, the Theocracy will be more inclined to let me have you de facto as you will have placed your trust in your savior." He gave her a pointed look and smiled at her. "You will, of course, be gagged for those proceedings. Then it will be back up to Taylorsville where you belong, you Trollip."

"I will never stop fighting you!" Lucy said. "The Consortium won't let you get away with this." She managed to pull back hard enough to get him to stop walking for a moment.

"The Consortium," he sneered, turning on her, "will have forgotten all about this little incident once your Jaeger and

112

that damn accountant out there are dead. I haven't forgotten about Mr. Wolverton costing me the Carmichaels as well. While your brother would've had Miss Charity out there, I would've had my pick of her sisters once they were delivered to me. But then she had to go run off to Elysium and pick up that damn bean counter." He jerked her arm again. "Now let's go, *wife!*" He pulled her outside as they headed for his vehicle.

The raider airship now hovered high overhead and raiders were rappelling down on dropped ropes. They opened fire on the guests, many shots going high over heads to get them to duck or dive for cover. Their shots were expertly placed as they gunned down a few of the men while avoiding the women. Other raiders came in behind the first line to start scooping ladies up who were in anguish that their men had been shot. Anderson continued to boldly march forward until one shot came too close for comfort.

"Not me, you fools!" he bellowed at them. "Them!"

It was apparently the wrong thing to say as more shots came their way, causing Anderson to yelp in alarm and loosen his grip on Lucy. Lucy took the opportunity to bolt. She had to find Gabriel or Deacon.

CHAPTER 15

Gabriel came out the front doors with his arm cannon up and firing. The raiders that were out in the open as they charged the estate were gunned down in short order. Those lucky enough to have been farther back ducked under cover and started to return fire.

Gabriel could easily take out any single raider. However, with multiple raiders firing back an assortment of beamers and rudimentary gunpowder firearms, he couldn't have such luck. He knelt behind a long masonry planter that came up to his waist and took aim.

He wasn't alone—there was a man cowering behind it as well. At first, Gabriel paid him no mind until he saw who it was.

"Anderson?"

Gabriel looked around and then grabbed the little weasel of a man by the scruff of the neck. "Where's Lucy?" he shouted through his armor's speakers.

Before the old raider airship arrived, Gabriel had been watching the exchange between Anderson and Lucy from a distance. When he looked back, they'd disappeared.

"I don't know! I was escorting her to safety when the attack began and she ran off!" Anderson whined. "Don't let them take me," he begged Gabriel, tugging at his powered arm.

Gabriel slugged him with a vicious right cross to dislodge him. Anderson crumpled to the ground, unconscious.

"Been wanting to do that for months now," Gabriel muttered as he got his head back into the fight.

***

Inside was bedlam as raiders came in from the north wing, having found that the side entrances preferable to the front doors. Lucy looked in every room for any sign of Gabriel or Deacon. Hell, at this point she'd settle for that accountant. Guests flooded back inside to lock themselves into whatever room they could find. Raiders were shooting men and taking women captive without discrimination. At one point, she even saw Lady Vickers crying over her husband's prone and bloody body right before two raiders dragged her off kicking and screaming.

Lucy searched up and down the halls of the north wing, calling for both her Jaeger and her master. Lucy found herself all the way at the end of the wing and so she turned back, only to be cornered by a single raider who was leering at her. He holstered his weapon and walked toward her. Cornered and desperate, Lucy grabbed the closest weapon she could find—an old Calvary sabre mounted on the wall, which had been in the Michaelson family since before the Great War. The sword was heavier than she'd expected and it dropped straight to the floor with a loud *thud* despite her two-handed grip on the handle.

The raider stopped in his advance and laughed at her fumbling about with the antique weapon. It proved to be his downfall as Lucy wasted no time in swinging it up toward his head as much as she could. It embedded into the side of his neck and he stood there with a shocked look on his face as he started to bleed out. He tried to raise his pistol, but Lucy used all of her might to drag the sabre out of his neck to make a clumsy strike at his hand. This time, the sabre didn't cut so much as it wound up breaking his wrist.

Before the raider could do anything, he dropped to his knees. Lucy could see that he was losing blood at an alarming rate. Without any further theatrics, his eyes glazed over and he pitched backward, dead. Letting out a roar of anguish at being attacked, she hit him again, and again, and again. She put forth all the anger, shame, and rage that had been pent up inside of her for months now. With a fury that she'd never known existed inside of her, Lucy pummeled the raider until he was a bloody heap on the carpet.

Maybe it was Anderson finally making his move on her that did it. Finally, she stopped with the saber up over her head as she was poised to strike again. Lucy stood over his lifeless body, her naked chest heaving from the sudden spike of adrenaline coursing through her system. Her mind worked feverishly as it processed what had just happened.

As reality hit her, she pitched over and retched into one

corner… she'd just killed someone! Afterward, she wiped the tears and snot from her face the best she could. She wasn't safe in the estate now. She heard the raiders all around the mansion, the cacophony of battle punctuating that fact, and the cries of the wounded and recently abducted, Lucy started to get the feeling that nowhere on the estate grounds would be safe. But, where could she go? Hearing the telltale sound of a Gatling beamer outside, she picked up her newfound saber and dashed down the hallway.

Two more raiders came out of a side room and ran right into her. The three of them fell into a tangle of limbs, her weapon bouncing out of reach.

"Grab her!" one of them said. "We gotta get back to the airship. The Dixie Air Corps is coming in!"

Lucy had started to get back up right as she saw the hand of the second one coming down to slap her hard across the face, momentarily dazing her. When she came to, she was being bounced up and down, her hands and ankles now bound. She realized she was being carried over one of the raiders' shoulders as they dashed out of the estate.

"Gabriel!" she cried out as she was hustled off.

***

Gabriel's blood froze as he heard Lucy's anguished scream from somewhere off to his right.

"Lucy!" he breathed in horror. He stopped firing out the front door and charged down the hall that led to the north wing.

His radio crackled. "Messenger, Emancipator here. I just landed in the front lawn. The raiders are pulling back with prisoners in tow."

"Already?" Gabriel was shocked—they hadn't been here that long.

"Well, I took the liberty of calling the Dixie Air Corps," Emancipator admitted. "The *James Longstreet* is in the area and they're already closing in to assist us. They've already issued a challenge to them. The raiders will be easily outmatched in that dilapidated thing they call an airship."

Gabriel burst out of one of the side servant's doors and

was met with a hail of gunfire. He lifted his gauntlet toward the retreating raiders. Reaching up behind his helmet with his right hand, he toggled the magnification optics. They slid down the front of his visor slits and his vision zoomed in for easier targeting.

"Lucy!" he called out as he watched her being carried away over the shoulder of one raider.

"That lady you've been doing the investigation for is here?" Emancipator asked.

Ignoring him, Gabriel gunned down any raider within his range while running full tilt for his girl. He wasn't about to let her be taken.

"Gabe!" Emancipator shouted. "Watch out for those airship guns!"

"Ah, shit!" Gabriel planted his feet and skidded to a halt, looking up at the raider airship that loomed above him. It was just in time, too, as the starboard guns, already pointed downward, started firing. They impacted into the ground just in front of him and, had he still been running, he would've been vaporized. Instead, the explosions knocked him backwards. He pinwheeled in the air as he was thrown twenty feet back. He rolled with the hard landing, coming to rest up against the wall.

"Get up! Get up!" Emancipator was now next to Gabriel, hauling him to his feet.

"I gotta get her!" Gabriel struggled in his grip, though Emancipator's brute strength nearly immobilized him.

"How far out is the *Longstreet*?" Gabriel asked, wincing.

Emancipator's helmet shook back and forth, telling him that it wasn't any time soon.

"We have to do something!"

"Calm down and take a deep breath, man. We'll link up with the *Longstreet* when they get here and we'll evaluate options," Emancipator instructed and then grabbed Gabriel by the shoulders and shook him. "You get me, Jaeger?" he demanded.

"Yeah...," Gabriel said, regaining his wits. There were others here that needed tending to. At least the captured guests were safe as far as the physical sense of the word went. "Let's go see how bad it is and report this in."

117

Deacon and Lucas had quickly constructed a makeshift bunker to protect themselves from the raging fight and didn't emerge until the raiders were in the now-ruined courtyard. Deacon looked around, astounded. Now the place looked like a warzone from the Great War—he couldn't believe it. Deacon had to hand it to the accountant—the number of dead bodies on the ground was a testament to Lucas' skill with a beamer. Lucas ran over to his wife who he'd thrown to the ground behind a table he upended when the fighting started. She nodded that she was okay and took his offered hand of assistance.

"Well...," Lucas said, glancing over at Deacon, "I must admit that you sure do throw one helluva party, Michaelson."

Deacon frowned and then ignored him as Gabriel walked up with another Jaeger in full armor. "You two okay?" Gabriel asked.

"Yes," Deacon said and nodded. "Thanks to you and your friend here." He stretched his hand out to the newly arrived Jaeger. "My thanks. I'm Deacon Michaelson."

"Lincoln Powell, Jaeger Emancipator," he replied, gingerly shaking Deacon's hand through the power armor.

"And this," Gabriel added, gesturing to Lucas, "is Lucas Wolverton, Consortium accountant out of New Eden."

"You chose an interesting place to go vacationing, sir," Lincoln quipped. "Usually people go down to Elysium for getaways, not the other way around."

"Eh," Lucas said with a shrug. "I heard that the Bay of Mississippi was nice this time of year... warm, slightly cloudy, and only a small percentage of a hail of gunfire."

Lincoln laughed. "Ha! I like him!"

"So, what's your plan now, gentlemen?"

Gabriel looked around as shell-shocked guests collected their wits and scattered belongings. "We've got to clean up, see to the wounded, and report this to the Consortium."

Lucas waved them off. "Consider it called in. I can see to that here. Oh, don't look at me like that. I might be a mere accountant to you high and mighty Jaegers, but I'm still a Consortium official, right? I'll handle cleanup. You two should go after those raiders." They all looked up again with nervous anticipation as the sound of another airship's engines filled the air. Lucas looked at them. "Backup?"

"Yeah," Gabriel confirmed.

"Then get yer butts up there and get going already. Go! I'll take care of things here!" Lucas admonished them, shooing them on with a wave of his hands."

"With all due respect, sir," Lincoln said politely but tersely, "but how do you suggest we do that? Other than charging into Lo'Rock with guns blazing, that is. We have no idea where they went!"

Gabriel's eyes locked on the small metal baton that hung from Deacon's belt. "Actually... I think I have an idea on how we can do that."

CHAPTER 16

What little remained from Lucy's maid's uniform was stripped off her the moment she was brought into the dimly lit cargo hold of the raider's airship. As a slave, she'd grown so accustomed to non-stop nudity that it didn't faze her in the least bit... unlike many of the noblewomen who'd been captured. Lucy counted about thirty women who had been caught before the raiders hastily retreated.

"You! Slave," one of the prim and proper ladies with vibrant red hair and blonde streaks snapped, pointing at Lucy as she was dropped onto the floor of the hold. It was Feckla, and her constant stream of tears had smeared her makeup something awful. "Your ilk is used to this sort of treatment! Tell them that *we* are to be handled differently!"

Lucy couldn't believe the nerve of the noblewoman. The high and mighty lady was now demanding that Lucy do something so she could be spared the indignity of being rendered naked like everyone one. She watched as many others were stripped down and affixed with metal collars

Lucy couldn't help but let out a hollow laugh. "You're a bitch, you know that?" Lucy glared at her. "Where were *you* when I needed help? Huh? Where were you when my family was in need? Where were you when I got railroaded?" She lifted her own collar in emphasis. "We're even now! We're equals now, so you get off your damn high horse *Lady* Vickers!"

"Heh, the little iSlave from the Theocracy knows her place already," a raider said as he came up to start cutting the dress, corset, and undergarments off Feckla, despite her squawks of protest. "The sooner you learn yours, the happier you'll be."

When he was done, the former Lady Vickers had a stunned expression on her face and a crude, but effective, iron collar around her neck.

"W-why?" she mewed pitifully, tugging at her new collar in a futile gesture, as the raider moved on to the next person. "Why didn't you do anything?" She was now crying anew.

Lucy glared at her. "Why didn't *you* when *I* needed it? It sucks, doesn't it? To be rendered naked and helpless as you're led off to your fate?" She crossed her arms and rested them on her knees, ignoring a slight twinge of pain that shocked her at the base of her neck. Burying her face in her arms, she ignored Lady Vickers' hysteric cries about being captured by "low life ruffians."

Screw her, Lucy thought bitterly. *I don't care if she just lost her husband or not. Let her get a taste of what I went through.*

***

"They must be pushing that old airship to its limits," Captain Atticus Sevier, commander of the D.A.C.S. James Longstreet muttered as he looked at a map of the area, his native Tennessee drawl accenting his irritation. "That, or they're not taking the direct route back. Helm!" he barked out over his shoulder. "Take us out over the Bay of Mississippi and begin search pattern close to Lo'Rock. We'll find that raider airship if it's the last thing we do."

"Aye, sir!" the helmsman echoed back, turning the massive wheel to the left to put the *Longstreet* into a tight turn.

"Contact! Wrecks off the port bow! Looks like Michaelson Family gunships!" a spotter reported.

"So much for Deak's fleet being ready...," Gabriel muttered as he and Lincoln were off to one side of the tactical table. Lincoln dictated numbers from an owner's baton while Gabriel entered them into a scanner, each number going in with a click as they were dialed in. "No need to do a search—we can find them easily enough," Gabriel told the captain without looking up.

Atticus eyed them. "Really? How's that?"

"Every iSlave's collar is embedded with a transponder in the event they run off since they are, essentially, criminals," Lincoln explained after giving the last number to Gabriel. He tossed the baton over to the captain who bobbled it slightly before getting control of it. "The number on the side of an owner's baton matches both the contract number and the transponder ID number that is on the collar so that we can enter it into our scanners to track them down."

"The Michaelsons' only iSlave, Lucy Spence, was taken," Gabriel pointed out. "She'll lead us right to their airship."

"Which, in turn, will lead us to the rest of the hostages," the captain said, getting the Jaeger's plans at last. "Where do we need to go, then?"

Gabriel looked up at the massive directional compass that loomed over the main viewport, which gave the crew an impressive panoramic view of the sky. He confirmed the direction with what the scanner said.

"Have your helm come back to starboard to fly two-eight-seven, true," he said, "and prepare them for battle."

***

Deep within the cargo hold of the raider airship, Lucy jerked upright as soon as she felt the electrical shock on the back of her neck intensify. It subsided for a minute before she felt the small jolt again. *What on earth is going on?* She felt back behind her neck and was shocked a third time. She remembered the words of those Consortium officials when she was auctioned off: *If you ever attempt escape, the Jaegers will home in on you. You'll feel a jolt in the back of your neck that will remind you of this. Once you return within proper range of your owner's control baton, the jolts will cease. You'll more than likely be punished further, but at least the small shocks of electricity on the back of your neck will have stopped...*

I'm being tracked, Lucy realized. Someone back at her master's estate must have noticed that she was gone and initiated the collar's tracking device. She wanted to jump up and clap with glee but knew that would draw too much attention. No, for the time being, she'd endure the tiny little twinges of pain. She didn't want to be separated from the collar out of fear of being permanently lost within the Wastelands. She'd heard enough horror stories to not want that to happen. Lucy wanted to be rescued, and even if she was singled out from the rest of the group, she'd be the one found first.

122

For some reason, that gave her a perverse sense of justice to see these aristocratic high-and-mighty people be brought down with her. *Serves them right for hanging me and my family out in our greatest hour of need,* she thought bitterly.

Suddenly, the entire deck pitched down and to the left, sending all the newly captured women tumbling. At first, Lucy wondered if they were under attack and then realized that they must be getting close to their destination.

"Gabe...," she muttered under her breath. "You'd better be on your way."

***

"Tallyho!" Atticus cried out triumphantly as he saw their quarry through the spyglass. "It's the *Airship Oculus* and she's already going in for a landing in Red Fields."

"That's one of Frost's trio," Lincoln noted as he came up to the domed forward glass of the bridge. His goggles zoomed in automatically to look at the landing airship. "Damn, I would've loved to have bagged the *Theurgy* while they're on the ground now that we're going to get the *Oculus* and the *Henosis* is ours now, too. The *Theurgy* is Auctor Frost's pride and joy, unlike that bag of bolts down there."

"One thing at a time, hero," Gabriel noted. He looked at the captain. "How do you want to play this?"

Atticus thought it over before answering. "We don't want to damage the cargo holds on the lower decks, but we don't want them taking off, either." He turned on his heel and faced the bridge crew. "Helm! Hard over to starboard! Engines! All stop! Side drift us and bring the port guns to bear! Aim for the tanks!"

The bridge crew repeated and relayed the orders. The *Longstreet* pulled itself over to the right, listing slightly until the ballast's pumps righted them as they drifted to the left.

"Gunners report target in sight!" the chief gunner reported back.

"And this is why you don't sacrifice altitude in an airship fight...." Atticus grinned savagely at the Jaegers. "Portside guns! Fire!" he roared.

Twenty guns along the left side of the airship fired in succession, the percussion of the cannons sounding like a string of firecrackers as they went off. Explosions lit up on the ground and along the back spine of the *Oculus*. Plumes of reddish brown gas shot out of punctures in the tisigen tanks like geysers. The raider airship plummeted downward fast, clearing the last hundred feet to the ground like a rock.

"Engines! Starboard docking engines! All full!" Atticus now called out as he moved to the portside dome of the bridge to observe the battle better. "Portside guns! Secondary targets—I want those guard towers gone!" He pointed to his helmsman. "Bleed off the tisigen tanks and take us down slow. Keep our portside to the enemy and be ready to flip us around when the guns need to be cycled."

"Aye, sir!" the helmsman responded as he carried out his orders in conjunction with the engine officer.

Atticus gestured to the hatch on the portside of the bridge. "Gentlemen, I believe this is your stop?"

Gabriel and Lincoln traded grins before slapping their helmets down onto their powered armor. "Thanks for the ride, Captain," Gabriel said, his speakers now making his voice sound mechanical.

"Just get our women back." Atticus nodded to them as he motioned for one of his crew to open the hatch.

The hatch flew open and the two Jaegers jumped out into the dark void beyond.

CHAPTER 17

"Go! Go! Go!" raiders shouted as they hauled naked women up to their feet and started shoving them toward one of the side doors of the cargo hold that was now open to the outside.

Lucy had lost her bearings when the ship suddenly dropped and hit the ground hard. She'd tumbled about and hit her head on the floor. The next thing she knew, she was being picked up and pushed toward the door right behind Feckla. There were more booms from cannon fire and explosions all around them. She didn't know who was shooting at them, but she had the good sense to not want to be on this airship anymore.

When her bare feet hit dirt, there was another raider there to redirect her. She fell into line with the rest of the running women and raiders who were herding them away from the crippled airship. Unable to help herself, she looked back over her shoulder. High up in the sky was a massive Dixie Air Corps airship with the Stars and Cross emblazoned on its huge tailfin. That sight brought a smile to her face as it rained down death onto the raiders all around them. Guard towers and anti-airship emplacements exploded around the landing area as Dixie let the raiders know just how much they were displeased with so many of their daughters being taken.

Lucy caught sight of two bright lights in the sky descending from the Dixie airship. She tried to get a good look as they came ever closer. Then the raiders were forcing her down a side alleyway covered in sand among ramshackle huts and ruined buildings. To her horror, she realized that they were splitting them up as Feckla had been directed down a different alley. It looked like they were taking every other woman and making them go in different directions. Her eyes flicked up as gun-toting loud med herded her down the dark, debris-filled alley. The streaks of light bent her way and she saw their outlines finally. *Jaegers*. Gabriel and another Jaeger were indeed tracking her.

When they broke into an open square of buildings, Lucy got an idea and intentionally tripped over a brick that was jutting out. She tumbled to the ground and took the five girls behind her down with her. The raiders in the back of the line with them shouted for them to get to their feet. Being at the bottom of the pile, Lucy was the last one up. Despite being covered in dirt with a painfully bruised foot, she smiled at the raider who had a hold of her.

"You're dead," she said sweetly.

He gave her a confused look right as one of the Jaegers landed behind him.

***

Gabriel wished he had armor that had a flasher on it so that he could record the raider's dumbfounded look posterity. He'd released Lucy and turned in place, looking up at Gabriel with wide-eyed fright. Gabriel raised his arm cannon and Lucy dove to the side, out of the way. The raider fell the ground, headless, a moment later.

Gabriel looked at Lucy. "You okay?" he asked through his speaker.

"About time you showed up!" Lucy admonished him. "They've been splitting us up into groups," she said and nodded in two different directions since her hands were manacled behind her back.

Flicking his right arm out, Gabriel's Jaeger blade came out from the top of his suit's forearm. "Turn around," he told her. She did and he swiped with the blade, severing the chains. "That'll have to do for now," he said as he moved on to the next bound woman that got caught up in the pileup with Lucy. Movement caught his eye and his armor registered the threat of a weapon pointed his way. He leveled his arm cannon and fired, killing the attacker instantly. Then he went back to freeing the girls. "Messenger to *Longstreet*, send skimmers to my location. Six for pickup."

"Already heading your way, Messenger," the communications officer on the *Longstreet* replied crisply. "Should be landing now."

Gabriel turned and saw the skimmer longboats now touching down. Marines from the airship jumped out with beamer rifles at the ready for any threats. Skirmishes broke out as they found hostile raiders. The raiders, not expecting a full-out invasion, broke and ran, leaving the Dixie Marines with the brief battlefield. A Marine in his dark blue-white battle tunic and black combat pants ran up and saluted a sergeant from what Gabriel saw by the stripes on his uniform cuffs. "Sir! The captain sent us down to assist," he reported.

Nodding his helmet, Gabriel pointed at Lucy and the five other women. "Get the them out of here and keep the area secure. Keep this one safe," he said, nodding to Lucy. "She's a key Consortium witness. If any harm comes to her, you'll have me to answer to personally!"

"I'll ensure her safety with my life, sir!" the sergeant saluted again before taking Lucy by the arm and leading her toward the longboats.

"Emancipator!" Gabriel keyed his radio as the Marines led the women off to the safety of the longboats. "We've got a problem."

"Yeah, I figured. I got five secured and I'm following a group of ten north into the city and the raiders are splitting them up even more," Lincoln radioed back. "This is gonna turn into a shit-show real fast."

Atticus broke into the conversation. "Gentlemen, the *Thomas Jackson* is coming up from the south to assist. They're already launching longboats to help secure the beachhead. You'll have more men on the ground to assist with the search shortly."

Gabriel looked in the direction indicated and saw that the sister military airship to the *Longstreet* was slowly chugging up the coast of the bay. Pinpricks of lights dropped from both sides of the massive armored behemoth where the longboats were dropped and powered away from their mothership. Its massive guns were already shelling gun emplacements on the ground and picking off smaller raider airships as they tried to launch to meet the new threat.

"Never thought I'd say this, but thank God for Dixie...," Gabriel muttered.

"Amen, brother," Lincoln agreed.

Doing some mental math, Gabriel figured that there were at least nine women in his general vicinity and he'd lost time getting the first six rescued. Every second counted—the deeper the raiders got into this small bayside town, the better the chance for them to further split up with their prizes and disappear. If they continued moving northwest, they'd eventually be out of Red Fields and up into Lo'Rock itself and then they'd be gone pretty much for good.

Engaging his thrusters, Gabriel took to the rooftops, clicking the searchlights on his suit to pierce the darkness as he tried to keep up with the fleeing raiders. Behind him, an explosion lit up the night as the *Longstreet* turned her guns onto the crippled *Oculus*, finishing the raider airship once and for all.

"Captain!" Gabriel growled into the radio. "There could've been hostages still on that airship!"

"Hardly," Atticus replied dryly. "The last person was out a couple of minutes ago when we launched our longboats. Messenger, we have all our spotters up here looking for the women. You have a big group heading due west to try and throw you off. Emancipator, you're going to want to go north by northwest from where you are. If you hit your thrusters, you might be able to get them as they break out of the town."

Gabriel and Lincoln both acknowledged the call outs. Cutting to the left, Gabriel ran and power hopped across the rooftops. Sporadic gunfire and beamer fire came his way from the few raiders left as they tried to bag a Jaeger. Gabriel hardly paid any attention to them as shots pinged and glanced off his armor. He picked off a couple on the fly while running by them as he searched for his main quarry.

A couple blocks later, Gabriel caught up with the bulk of the raiders. Two of them tossed their captive women down, turned, and held their ground against the advancing Jaeger. Gabriel hit the thrusters again and power jumped to leap over their gunfire. He sliced at the one to his right and fired his cannon at the one to his left as he landed in front of them. They fell to the ground, dead.

"Stay here!" he ordered the frightened and cowering women as he sent up a flare from the backpack of his armor. "*Longstreet*, *Jackson,* sending a flare up. Two to pick up at this location."

He didn't wait for a response from either airship before he continued on.

***

Lincoln planted an armored boot onto a raider's chest. The raider had had the nerve to engage him in hand to hand combat, which resulted in Lincoln tossing him off his back and to the ground. The raider, who had been all brave and badass five seconds ago now cowered in fright. As much as he wanted to blow a hole in the man's skull, Lincoln stayed his hand. Instead, he reversed his rifle and knocked the guy out with the stock. He then hit his thrusters to get up in the air and ahead of the raiders that the *Longstreet* indicated.

He found a group of five that had yet to split up. Lincoln swore under his breath—this might bet the last few that he'd be able to get as they were now out of space. Ten klicks down the road across a barren stretch of old highway was Lo'Rock, and Lincoln could see heavy raider airships disengaging from their tower berths to turn their noses his way.

"Messenger, we're outta time, man. Lo'Rock is launching their airships to join the party."

It wasn't his fellow Jaeger who answered, but the D.A.C.S *Thomas Jackson* as it continued chugging through the air over Lincoln's head, ponderously turning to the left as it brought its guns to bear.

"Fear not, Jaeger Emancipator," the captain of the *Jackson* radioed down to him. "Just like the stone wall of our namesake, we'll hold the line for you as you liberate our women."

To punctuate the point, the *Jackson* opened with full broadsides, hurling out its volley of death toward the oncoming raider airships.

Another voice cut in as a pair of Devastators screamed though the air past the *Jackson* to give a faster raider airship a full spread of beamer cannon fire.

"Y'all having fun here and you didn't even invite me to the party...," Coleton Muller admonished him from the lead aircraft. "Shame on all y'all!"

Lincoln threw his head back and laughed. "Glad you're here to back us up, Intruder," he said. "Who's your wing-man?"

"Eh, just some jerk that I picked up along the way,"

Coleton said flippantly. "He happened to be in the area with his ride."

As much as Lincoln wanted to press the issue, he didn't; he had ladies to save. He ignored the air battle developing overhead and caught up to the fleeing group of raiders. Upraising his rifle, he caught one in the back with a snap shot, sending him screaming to the ground in pain. The seven remaining raiders scattered, putting the five women into various hiding spaces behind walls or underneath the sparse underbrush. Lincoln looked back and forth, not wanting to fire when he couldn't see the captives.

Almost as if the captain of the airship could read his mind, the *Jackson* lit up the area with their massive searchlights all pointing down on his location. Now Lincoln could see them all. He shouldered his rifle and flicked both of his wrists downward, producing his small Jaeger blades from the tops of both gauntlets. Then, using his armor's superior speed, he charged the two in front of him who happened to be standing close together, driving his electrified blades through their chests.

A third raider was nearby and Lincoln lunged for him, taking the man's wrists off in a single swipe when he squared himself to fire his beamer. He went to his knees, howling in pain before Lincoln gave him a savage kick to the head. The other four started firing and Lincoln continued running around the big circle that they'd created, hacking and slashing until they were all dead on the ground, their blood mixing with the hot sand.

An explosion caused by a beam of light on the wall just over his head made him duck. He looked up to see one of the smaller raider airships, a Cutter-Class, had slipped through the barrage of cannon fire from the *Jackson* and the two Consortium Devastators. Lincoln stiffened as he stared down the two massive forward barrels of the Cutter while they charged for the next shot that'd kill him.

"Get up and run!" he shouted thorough his speakers, hoping it would get the women to scurry for safety. He fired flares behind him to signal for pickup while he pulled his beamer rifle out and started taking potshots at the Cutter.

The Cutter suddenly exploded, crashing to the ground in

a fiery wreck. From behind it, the black Devastator flew through the trail of smoke that billowed upwards, doing a victory barrel roll in the process.

"Dude...," Lincoln breathed with relief as he watched the airplane fly by. "I don't know who you are, but you have my thanks."

"Don't worry about it," the mysterious pilot radioed back amid a burst of static. "Just get those women back to the Michaelson estate and that'll be thanks enough.

CHAPTER 18

While the *James Longstreet* and the *Thomas Jackson* held their newfound gains on the far side of the Mississippi Bay, their skimmer longboats flew the newly liberated women back to the Michaelson estate with the two Consortium Devastators escorting.

Lucy had heard the men talking about a 'Butcher's Bill' of the dead, wounded, and missing. Twenty Dixie Marines and thirty-two airship crewmen died in the exchange over Red Fields with another hundred wounded. All to save her and seventeen other maids and noblewomen. Twelve of the captured women were still missing and presumed lost to the raiders until the Consortium could mount a Jaeger expedition into the Wastelands to track them down.

"Something on your mind, Miss?" the Marine sergeant asked her, looking at her with concern. He hadn't left her side since Gabriel ordered him to protect her, and from his demeanor, he was taking that job as if God himself had come down and given him the task. The sergeant had even gone so far as to break out the emergency blankets for her and the other naked women still burdened with shackles and collars.

"Just... thinking... that's all," Lucy admitted. "All this for a handful of women who are barely second-class citizens." She glanced at him. "Makes me wonder why."

"Mmmmm...." The sergeant nodded his understanding. "We sons and daughters of Dixie are a strange lot, I'll admit that. We promote the Lord's word in the One Book as being the right and just thing to follow and then we do something stupid like put other people down to subpar levels. After the Confederacy fell and went back to being Americans, we thought we'd put the evils of slavery behind us. Then, ain't life grand—America collapses under its own weight and here we are again, rehashing the old wounds until the Consortium steps in. Some say we're not much better than the old Confederacy in that we just went back to the old ways. I think that we're just a bit better off than before under either the Confederacy or the United States."

"Oh? How so?" Lucy asked, unable to keep the skepticism out of her voice.

"Sure, we might treat women a bit unfairly at times, but that's because we want to protect them in our own way. At the end of the day, we're all still Dixie. We all fight and die to protect what's ours and we'll be damned if any filthy, godless raider is gonna come in and take our ladies for their own depraved purposes." He shook his head. "Nosiree, not on our watch. We might not be perfect, but thus far we've outlasted the Confederacy and we're well on our way to outlast America by avoiding the mistakes of our forefathers."

"Hmmm...," Lucy grunted, adding something else to think about on the flight back home.

***

Upon returning to the Michaelson estate and overseeing the offload of the liberated women, Gabriel found Lucas Wolverton standing watch over Overseer Anderson in a makeshift prison inside the gazebo in the back courtyard. Lucas looked hot and sweaty in his suit with his black hair matted in places as if he'd just completed one hell of a workout.

"Glad to see you back," Lucas told him. "I just took over guard duty from your friend, Deacon. He tossed him in here on a citizen's arrest, saying that you were investigating him and didn't want him to, what was the words he used? Slither off like the snake he is? Anyway, Deacon is off checking on his staff and should be back any minute."

"Thanks, I appreciate the help." Gabriel took off his helmet, breathing in the fresh air, and nodded at him. "And thanks for calling in the air support from Atlanta. Intruder and his wingman were invaluable and saved Emancipator and five women's lives."

"All in a day's work," Lucas said and grinned. "So, what are we going to do about your boy here?" he asked, crossing his arms in thought, studying the overseer like a caged animal.

"I'd love to shoot him now and be done with it," Gabriel spat. His left arm with the arm cannon twitched upward

"Ah, ah, ah...," Lucas admonished him with a quick wag of his finger. "Legal proceedings," he reminded him. "We might be Consortium, but even we need evidence to execute in the field."

Gabriel growled and glared at Anderson, who took a step back inside his ad hoc cell. "I have more than enough evidence to bury him," he snapped. "Only problem is that I need to have a court convened and wait for legal proceedings like you say."

Lucas gave him a half shrug. "You're a Jaeger. You can always convene one out in the field if you have enough people to ensure due process."

A light went off in Gabriel's head. The accountant was right—he *could* convene a battlefield courtroom. He just needed enough people to do it. Gabriel wanted to smack himself upside the head for not thinking of it himself.

He keyed his radio. "Emancipator, where are ya?"

"Out front getting the last of the longboats off the ground so Intruder can land," Lincoln responded. "Why?"

"Because I have an idea and I need all the people I can get, that's why."

***

A little bit later, with the help of Deacon and his staff, they had rounded up the remaining guests who had not been evacuated to the nearby hospital for treatment, or to see to their loved ones who'd been injured or captured. Now, they would sit as a witness gallery. Gabriel stood in the middle of a quick and dirty courtroom in the middle of the back courtyard with Overseer Anderson shackled to a chair where the accused dais would normally be. He caught sight of Lucy in the back and gave her a smile and a wink. She gave him a brave smile in return.

Anderson, for his part, looked around, confused, constantly demanding to know what was going on until Lucas walked over and shoved a rag into his mouth to shut him up. The protests continued, but were at least a bit muffled now.

"What *is* going on?" Lincoln asked. "Why are you setting things up like this?"

"Because I want this over and done with tonight." Gabriel smiled cruelly toward Anderson and then said the words that everyone on the wrong side of the Consortium feared the most: "Court is now in session."

134

Anderson paled at the announcement and managed to spit out his cloth gag. "Y-You can't convene court and be both the prosecutor, advocate, and the judge!" he protested.

"I can't," Gabriel said, still smiling. "But, he can." He gestured toward Lincoln. "The honorable Jaeger Emancipator, presiding."

"Aw, man, why'd you have to drag me into this?" Lincoln grumbled. He caught Gabriel's sharp look and then rolled his eyes. "I can't be the judge; I know too much about the case. Best I can do is be the prosecutor. You can still be advocate for your girl, and let him," he nodded to Lucas, "be the judge. He's a Consortium employee."

"*Can* he even be a judge?" Anderson demanded. "I thought that you needed at least *three* Jaegers to convene a legal proceeding."

"Where the hell is Intruder when you need him?" Gabriel asked, looking around.

"He was up flying combat air patrol until the longboats left," Lucas answered. "He'll be a bit while he finds a place to land as the space I cleared out wasn't enough of a strip for him."

When Anderson saw that the Jaegers traded an uncertain look, he smiled. "That accountant can't be a judge, can he? Even if he could, he'd have to recuse himself because he's too close to the case as well," he crowed in triumph.

"Really?" Lucas chimed in with a curious cock of his head, his eyes narrowing. "What the hell does your case have to do with me?" A dawning look crossed his face. "Unless you were in league with Eddie Spence to help bring down the Carmichaels."

When Anderson clamped his mouth shut and his eyes went wide, he gave himself away. He'd said too much!

In turn, Lucas' eyes blazed with fury. "Court is now in session! The honorable Lucas Wolverton now presiding," he announced.

"Umm..., unfortunately, Overseer Anderson is correct in

this regard," Gabriel said. He hated to admit it, but the law had to be followed. "According to the Consortium, you do have to be a Jaeger in order to be a battlefield judge. I'm... sorry, sir." That was the truth because he wanted to be done with Anderson right then and there.

Lucas rolled his eyes and sighed. "Ah, fuck it. This time it's worth it." Lucas gave them a knowing smile. "Come 'ere. Lemme show you something." He motioned for them to come in close before reaching into his inner suit pocket and fetching out his credentials. He opened it for them to see his Consortium financial badge. He then flipped over a hidden panel to show something that no one expected—a cog-and-star Jaeger Badge with his true credentials. "These proceedings are now, of course, classified," he said in a low tone so that only they could hear him.

"Jaeger Shadow...," Gabriel breathed.

"Sir!" Lincoln stiffened and started to salute along with Gabriel. "We didn't know...."

Lucas frantically waved them down. "Don't fucking salute me here, you morons," he hissed in irritation. "There's only a handful of people who know I'm really up here in the Theocracy instead of down in Elysium and I'd like to keep that number down."

"Wait a second," Lincoln chimed in. "So were you in...."

"That black Devastator-II over Red Field and Lo'Rock with Intruder that saved your bacon? Yeah, that was me," Lucas said and nodded.

"Right... sorry," Lincoln said. He looked at his two fellow Jaegers. "Soooo, about this field trial?"

"We just say that there's a new regulation out or something so that we can keep the witnesses in the dark." Lucas looked past them at everyone within relative earshot. "Get on with it, you two," he ordered with a slightly louder voice

"You heard the man," Lincoln announced, louder this time, walking over to his ad hoc place as prosecutor. "Court is now in session. I, as prosecutor, defer to the primary witness' advocate for opening arguments." He motioned to Gabriel.

"Wait! You're telling me he can preside as judge now?" Anderson was aghast.

"New regs that the accountant just made us aware of," Gabriel replied casually.

"Don't I get an advocate as dictated by Consortium law?" Anderson now asked, trying to stall for time as he realized what was happening.

"Oh?" Gabriel interjected. "You mean like when you, Ladd, and Takacy railroaded Miss Spence into a rapid trial without any hope of getting an advocate herself? I know that Theocracy justice is swift and all, but normally an advocate is given to at least provide the semblance of law and order."

"Isn't there that Intruder chap here yet?" Anderson looked around for the Jaeger.

"Yeah," Coleton said as he ran up to the crowd, sounding a bit winded. "Had to park my ride farther down the road than I expected."

"Be my advocate!" Anderson demanded.

"Sorry, but I recuse myself on the grounds that I don't represent assholes," Coleton replied, flipping him off. "Besides, I participated in your investigation."

Anderson looked around for support and found none among the condemning looks of the people assembled. Gabriel got right up into his face. "Over the past two months, I've gone over every single court case of Takacy's that involved young women and in each instance, it was done so fast as to make sure that an advocate was not available for the accused, which pretty much guaranteed a conviction for them to a breeder farm... *your* breeder farm... because First Corinthians chapter fourteen, verse thirty-four is always cited at the beginning of the trials. Would you like to enlighten the court as to what that passage says?"

Anderson eyes darted from Gabriel to Lincoln and then over to Lucas. "Do I have to answer that?" he asked, looking from Lincoln, to Coleton, and then to Lucas.

"Yes," Lincoln said evenly, crossing his big, burly arms, the servos in his armor squeaking in the process. He regarded Anderson with a stern look. "If the court orders it, that is," he added with a side look to his boss.

Lucas nodded in solemn agreement. "The court so orders."

Sighing with resignation, Anderson looked down to the

ground. "Women are to be silent in the churches. They are not permitted to speak, but must be in submission as the law says."

"Which," Gabriel continued, "we all know that, in the Theocracy, courtrooms often double as a place of worship in which the presiding judge is the supreme God and ruler. And, so, it is generally accepted as the same status as a church since all their laws are based off the One Book. Therefore, women were unable to testify in their own defense without either an advocate there to speak for them or a male of their own household to grant them permission." Gabriel turned to Lucas and smiled. "Would the court like to hazard a guess as to who was on hand every single time, whose name is on official records I might add, to take the women off into immediate custody?"

"I would guess that would be the accused here, correct?" Lucas now openly glared at Anderson.

"Give the man a cigar!" Gabriel laughed. "So, Overseer Anderson, do you deny the fact that you've been paid off by gold by Auctor Frost, and that steady payments of gold have been going from your breeder farm directly to Judge Takacy's accounts down in Atlanta?"

Anderson's head snapped up in abject terror. "Those records are confidential!" he protested.

"Ah, yes, to everyone but the Consortium, that is," Coleton chimed in. "You see, your accounts were at the National Bank of Dixie, whose now late Director was recently implicated in illegal slavery practices along with Edward Spence the Third, recently executed for the same practices along with embezzlement and theft. We at the Consortium launched an all-out audit of all accounts in that bank and your name came up quite a bit in relation to payments made to Judge Takacy."

"Which," Lincoln now added, "went back to Anderson here in the form of young ladies for his breeder farm in which gentlemen of the Theocracy pay top coin for the privilege of having. You send what you don't want out to the Wastes in the form of those fake-ass raids where the raiders pay you off by dropping the gold in their wake." He shook his head in disgust. "Shit... paying for an inmate out of a breeder farm is

138

a helluva lot cheaper than buying one at public auction. Especially here in the Theocracy where dowries and bride prices are over the roof. It drops the prices to rock bottom, which devalues pretty much everything in the local economy. While I'm willing to stipulate that dowries and bride prices need to drop, killing an economy is just fucked up."

"Yeah, tell me about it," Lucas agreed. "You should've seen the bill I had to cover for Charity."

"Which our 'esteemed' overseer here bid on our girl Lucy when she opted for iSlave status. A list of bidders, per Consortium law, is available back at headquarters," Gabriel confirmed. "It's the ultimate money laundering and illegal slave operation. The money gets washed through the judge as 'donations' or 'payments to the court' for whatever reasons and the judge pays him back in the form of young ladies that he then charges mightily for. They both get rich and there is a fresh supply of women heading to the farm and the Wastes for the locals to sample and get a free bride out of. Their pockets are lined and everything is on the up and up as far as the Theocracy is concerned."

"But, where the Consortium is concerned," Lincoln said, seeing where Gabriel was going with this, "it's tantamount to illegal slavery operations as you are openly forcing women into that status." He glanced at Lucas. "I suspect, your Honor, that fate was going to be reserved for your wife had you not intervened at the right time as Overseer Anderson here has now been connected to the Spence case."

"You have no proof," Anderson said rather weakly.

"I have no proof... *here*," Gabriel corrected, "except for one star witness." He made a pointed look over toward Lucy. "Shall I get her up here to testify? I'm sure that she'll be more than happy to."

"She's not allowed to!" Anderson protested with a dignified and defiant lift of his chin. "She is not allowed to speak in the presence of men...."

"Unless she is given permission by her master," Deacon piped up from the crowd as he pushed his way to the forefront. "Which I so allow." He glared daggers at Anderson. "Is it true what the Jaegers here are saying? *Have* you been enslaving the women of our country against their will like

139

this?" When Anderson didn't answer, Deacon bit his thumb and spat at the ground at Anderson's feet. "You make me sick!" He twisted back around and beckoned. "Lucy! Get up here and tell them what you know!"

***

Lucy came up with the Dixie Marine sergeant still by her side acting as her escort. She was uncertain, but seeing both Deacon and Gabriel smile and nod their encouragement, she stepped forward. Even Lincoln, Coleton, and Lucas silently supported her with smiles. She could do this. She'd done this twice before. Why should now be any different? She took her place in the center to render her testimony.

"He... he said that he wanted me to be his wife to lay claim to whatever assets my family had left," she said and then related everything that Anderson had told her right as the raiders were attacking. Lucy left no part out and even supplied the connections between her brother and Overseer Anderson. Relief swept over her as she realized that she was able to supply the account, word for word, thanks to her upbringing.

"He even has a device on him which called the raiders here," she added, finishing her testimony.

"You can't honestly expect to believe the word of a *woman* in a moment of panic during an attack?" Anderson protested, sneering at Lucy.

"Ad Hominem attack!" Coleton called out, raising his voice. "No bearing in Consortium court!"

"We're supposed to believe her just like we're supposed to believe you, when you told me that you were escorting her to safety when I found you cowering behind the flower beds?" Gabriel challenged, pointing over to the stone that had given them both protection the previous night. "Besides, Theocracy women have a knack for memorization, recital, and dictation as they're often required to learn such skills when they have to memorize passages and poems out of the One Book." He smiled at Lucy, acknowledging her skill. He then walked over and fished out the transmitter. "Well, whaddya know? You *do* have a radio transmitter here keyed to a raider transmission."

140

He tossed it to Lincoln.

Lincoln examined the device. "Yup, this is one of the frequencies that Auctor Frost loves to use for his fleet," he confirmed.

Lucas shook his head, holding up a hand to forestall any further argument or discussion. "Doesn't matter. I find that enough grounds exist for the charge and that Jaegers Emancipator and Messenger have provided sufficient evidence to find the accused guilty of illegal slavery practices as well as colluding with raiders to force others into illegal slavery in this battlefield court." He pointed at Lucy. "Mr. Michaelson, get her out of here and get some clothes on her. She's returning home to Atlanta under our care. I hereby suspend her iSlave status pending an official order from both the Theocracy and the Consortium."

As Deacon guided Lucy away, he averted her head so that she didn't have to see what was about to happen.

***

Lucas waved a hand over toward the two Jaegers. "Carry out the sentence."

"With pleasure," Gabriel said, leveling his arm cannon at Anderson.

Lincoln and Coleton turned and squared themselves in line with Gabriel, pulled their beamer rifles from over their shoulders, and aimed.

The crowd hastily parted behind Anderson to avoid being in the path of the newly formed firing squad. Anderson had time to glance back to see the now empty space behind him before looking back and down the barrels of the weapons.

Inside the armor, Gabriel tightened his fist around the pressure trigger assembly while Lincoln and Coleton squeezed their triggers. Multiple beams of light went through Anderson's head and upper torso, killing him instantly.

"Court's adjourned," Lucas added dispassionately at the falling body.

141

CHAPTER 20

Flanked by Shadow and Emancipator in full battle armor, Gabriel led the way into one of the small side courtrooms in Atlanta. Gabriel was in his dress uniform while Shadow remained incognito by borrowing Gabriel's armor.

Up on the bench, Takacy droned on about the Theocracy's propriety standard for women while Ladd looked smug over at the prosecutor's table. A young, frightened woman stood alone on the dais as Takacy passed judgement on her.

Takacy's face fell at the sight of three Jaegers walking into his courtroom. A wave of startled whispered went through the audience. Ladd caught the judge's alarmed look, turned, and blanched as he saw them stop right behind his table. Emancipator clamped a brass, gauntleted hand on the man's shoulder.

"Prosecutor Ladd, you are under arrest for aiding and abetting illegal slave trafficking," he said, his voice cold and mechanical as it came out of the armor's speakers. "You have the right to remain silent, so shut the fuck up. You have the right to an advocate. If you can't afford one, I'll make sure I find a goddamn first year law student at the bottom of their class to represent you." He hauled Ladd up out of his seat and started dragging him out of the courtroom.

"What is the meaning of this?" Takacy demanded, standing up at his bench as his face turned red with anger. "We are in session here!"

"Not anymore," Gabriel beamed. He fished out a letter from his briefcase and held it up for all to see. "This is an order from the Regional Director of the Jaeger Corps and the Regional Director of the Consortium to take Judge Bartholomew Takacy into immediate custody and to suspend all of his pending cases." He placed it on the empty advocate table and pulled out another letter. "This is from the Internal Security Council of the Theocracy that was just signed in emergency session. This order places into immediate review all trials that Judge Takacy, Prosecutor Ladd, Overseer

Anderson, and five other Theocracy prosecutors were involved in."

That paper then joined the first and Gabriel pulled out a third. "This...," he said with a flourish, "is a joint order from the Theocracy of Dixie and the Consortium that officially overturns *Theocracy v. Lucille Spence*."

Over on the bench, Takacy quivered with rage. He snapped his fingers at the muscular bailiff off to the side. "Get them out of my courtroom!" he shouted, his face red and flushed with anger.

"Like hell," the bailiff snorted, crossing his arms in defiance while shaking his head. "I ain't going up against three Jaegers... especially when they have legal orders and two of them are in armor."

"Good man," Gabriel said and smiled at him. "I'd take the rest of the day off if I were you. While you're at it, take her back to her holding cell and make sure that she's taken care of with decency and dignity," he added, pointing to the confused, frightened girl on the dais.

The bailiff gave a small smile and a slight bow before taking the girl out a side door away from the courtroom.

"So, now what?" Takacy thundered, looking over to where Ladd was being shackled and pushed out of the courtroom by Emancipator. "We go to trial? I'll have to call my advocate."

Gabriel held up a single finger as he looked down into his briefcase. "Oh, yeah... you're gonna love this." He snapped his fingers dramatically as he pulled out another paper. "This is your termination order."

Takacy looked at him incredulously. "I'm being given my firing papers by you and not the courts, just like that?"

"Wrong kind of termination," Gabriel gave him an evil smile.

"I think," Shadow said, lifting the arm cannon of his armor, aiming right at Takacy's chest, "that we'll just skip the rest of the paperwork."

***

"Are you ready?" Gabriel asked Lucy softly as they stood

outside her old manor home. He looked at her with concern etched on his face.

Not for the first time since leaving Atlanta, Lucy stroked her bare neck as she stared up at the manor. After growing accustomed to the iron collar, she felt naked without it, despite the simple dress that Charity Carmichael had given her to wear until they got here.

"What's going to happen to it?" she asked as childhood and adolescent memories came rushing back.

"Well, the statute of limitations goes back a decade to the first family that has yet to have reparations made to it, which is my family, I'm get first claim to it." He looked up at the manor. "I personally don't want it, but if you do, then I won't hesitate to nab it for you."

Lucy shook her head. "No, this stopped being my home the moment daddy... no, *the Reverend*...," she corrected herself, no longer thinking of the man as her father, "the moment he kicked me out is when this stopped being my home."

"I have a place down in Elysium that you might like...." Gabriel grinned. "It's a nice little studio apartment overlooking the Havana Bay."

Lucy smiled. "A simple studio apartment sounds good... so long as you'll be there with me?"

"It's a date," he said, holding out his hand. "Ready?"

She took it and squeezed. "Ready."

They walked into the manor where a clockwork opened the door and showed them into the spacious living room that had been stripped of all but the basic living necessities. Lucy took one look around and shook her head sadly. "I'm going up to get my things," she told him.

"Stay there until I come and get you," he told her, "You...."

"Don't want to see this, yeah, you'd think I'd be used to this by now."

"If you were getting used to it, I'd worry about you." Gabriel gave her a peck on the cheek and watched her go back out to the grand staircase to go to her old room.

"Well, my boy," Reverend Edward Spence, Jr. said, beaming at Gabriel as he came in from the kitchen with arms open wide. "I got your missive that you were coming here, and what can I say? You did it! You freed my daughter from slavery and restored her to her rightful place at home. The prodigal son returns triumphant. If there is anything you want; you just name it and it shall be yours. A home? A wife, perhaps?" He gestured upwards toward Lucy's room. "My daughter is available if you want her hand in marriage. A good marriage to an old Theocracy family will do well to restore both of our houses."

"She's not a pawn for you to move around just because it's convenient for you," Gabriel ground out, squaring himself for this last fight in this case. "You've used her as a bait and switch for far too long and it ends here today."

Spence snickered at him. "You can't just waltz in here and dictate what I can and cannot do to my own daughter, even if you are a Jaeger."

"Yeah, but she's not your daughter anymore," Gabriel interjected, his voice taking on a dangerous tone as he got right up next to the man to the point that they were nearly in each other's faces. "Regardless that she's been of age for years now, *you* disowned her after your son's trial and execution to the point that she moved out on her own accord." He jabbed a finger in the air his way to emphasize the point. "As far as both the Theocracy and the Consortium are concerned, she's her own person and there's not a damn thing you can do about it."

"My boy...." Spence took on a fatherly smile. "Anything can be reversed. Just like you are the prodigal son returning, she would be the prodigal daughter returning. You two can be rightfully married just like you were originally intended to be, and you'll take your place as my heir. All will be right in the world once again."

"You just don't get it, do you?" Gabriel didn't match his jubilant attitude. Instead, he simply held up a single piece of paper. "All I want right now is to serve you with this," he said evenly, though he glared at Spence. He laid it onto the table next to them and took a step back, drawing his beamer. "The Consortium has found you guilty of illegal slavery stemming over the past decade. The sentence is death and is to be carried out immediately upon serving of these papers."

Spence looked down at the paper that had *CONSORTIUM ORDER OF EXECUTION* emblazoned across the top with his name immediately underneath it. He looked back up at Gabriel.

"Is this a joke?"

"Do I look like I'm laughing?" Gabriel countered, aiming the beamer at Spence's forehead. "I've waited ten years for this moment since you sent me and my family up the river. My parents and my sister were sent up to Taylorsville where they all died. I just got lucky enough to get away before they got me as well."

"Your parents are dead now... that is true...," Spence admitted, his voice somber now that he had a beamer pointed at his head. "But your sister isn't."

Gabriel paused, his face furrowed with confusion. "What are you talking about? She, what?"

"You were told that she committed suicide the day that she got there. Yeah," Spence nodded. "But, think about that for a moment. That was a ploy to get you out into the open so that we could nab the last McKibben who had claim to the fortune, the land, and the military assets. Imagine my surprise when you did an end around us and gave the assets to the damn fucking Michaelsons and skipped on out to Elysium. No, your sister is alive... last I heard, anyway. She was traded by Anderson to his people over in the Wastelands."

A torrent of emotions washed over Gabriel. Everything he'd been led to believe for ten years had been a lie. His jaw clenched and his hand shook with rage. He glared daggers at Spence as his finger went from the side of the trigger guard to wrap around the trigger itself.

"Wait!" Spence cried out, stumbling backwards over a fainting couch with an outstretched hand. "Don't you even want to know where she is? I can even give you Auctor Frost's hideout that's far out west where she was last seen!"

"I don't care if I have to hire outlaws like Cheyenne or

146

the Angel to track her down. I'll fucking find her my own way without any help from the likes of you," Gabriel snarled as he pulled the trigger.

***

Lucy paced back and forth in her room, wringing her hands nervously. It felt odd to her, being back in a normal corset and dress after spending a couple of months near naked or totally naked. As expected, she didn't have much left—just a couple of trunks full of her clothes that appeared to be tagged for sale. She changed quickly, folded up Charity's donation dress to put into one of the trunks, and then had what few clockworks were left in the house take them to Gabe's steam carriage outside. Now the room was empty and lonely as she waited.

A crack of beamer fire downstairs made her jump. Seconds later, she heard heavy footsteps coming up the stairs and down the hallway. She let out the breath she'd been holding when Gabriel opened the door.

"It's done...," he said with no trace of joy or satisfaction in his voice, which relieved her further. "The Spence family is now, officially, dissolved."

"Then let's get out of here, my love," Lucy said, crossing the room to him and pressing her body up against his. Craning her neck, she gave him a quick kiss. "There's nothing left for me here. I want to go home... with you."

Gabriel smiled and offered her the crook of his arm. She matched his smile and slipped her arm through his, allowing him to lead her down the stairs, out the door, and off into the future.

EPILOGUE

Out in the far west, in the outskirts of the desert city known as Vegaston, the Angel of Death pushed his way through the double swinging doors of the Lucky Lady saloon and hotel. He looked particularly beat up today and his hard face belied his equally foul mood. His boots thudded on the wooden floorboards as he crossed the space to the bar, going for his usual stool that someone else occupied. Other patrons made a point to scramble out of his way, but the oblivious man at the bar paid no mind to him. Even the barmaid tried to shoo the drunk patron off to make way for Angel.

"I'll leave when I'm damn good and ready," the man said with his speech slightly slurred. "Whoever he is can go sit elsewhere!"

The Angel paused, frowning as he looked down the line of patrons who were belly up against the bar. They all cleared out so fast that the stools were knocked down in their wake.

"You all get your asses back here and pick these up! You're not making the barmaid's lives any fucking easier by running outta here like a fucking dust devil," he hollered at them before they could reach the door. They all skidded to a halt and meekly turned back in place to tidy up before making their hasty retreat under his hard gaze.

Now the drunk patron turned as he realized who was behind me. "A-A-Angel! I did-didn't know you's was back in town!" he stammered with a hiccup.

"Now you know, and I think that you've had enough to drink this evening," the Angel told him.

"Yassir! You are right, sir!" The drunk tripped over in the legs of the barstool, crashing to the ground. He got up, righted the stool, dusted it off, and made tracks out of the saloon.

"You know," the barmaid admonished him from behind him, "You drive off good business when you do that... bad mood or not."

"So, fucking sue me, Adeline," he said, cordially tipping his hat to the redheaded barmaid before setting it on the bar.

"The usual, if you please?"

Adeline McKibben shook her head as she turned in place, grabbing a shot glass and a bottle of whiskey. She placed them both down in front of him, pouring him a quick drink.

"You should go easy on Old Willie there," she told him, crossing her arms and glaring at him as she leaned against the bar. "He just gave me a tidbit that the town council up in Delmar is selling out to the Gatlings to fuel their airships. You might be able to get up there before the gang comes down from Yellowstone."

"Huh...," the Angel grunted as he downed his drink, savoring the fire that dropped to his belly. "Might have to deal with them later since the snows are coming early this year in Yellowstone. They're not gonna fly those dilapidated airships of theirs anytime soon, and I have a lot on my plate at the moment."

"Oh? Like what?' Adeline asked with an arched eyebrow.

He smiled at her. "Like you." He held out his gloved hand to her. "If you're ready for the second part of my usual, that is?"

She gave him an incredulous smile as she shook her head. "As always, I'm yours for the evening to do with as you please."

"And please you I do," the Angel said as she came around the bar. He hooked her neck with his hand over the back of her iSlave iron collar and pulled her into a passionate kiss before leading her by the hand up the nearby staircase and into his room where he proceeded to give her one mind blowing orgasm after another until they both passed out asleep from exhaustion.

The End

Made in the USA
Columbia, SC
25 January 2024

30208740R00085